SLAVE SHIP

The electronic brain machines have broken codes, translated one human language into another, and have now turned their memory banks to the problems of deciphering animal languages. The first practical application of this is to tell the sheep to eat the weeds in the potato patch, but to leave the potatoes alone. This however, is only the beginning.

The nature of animals is that they are expendable. When a prolonged "cold" war has created a manpower shortage so acute that Boy Scouts are being drafted, the navy, characteristically resourceful, turns to other available material. To an Annapolis graduate, veteran of several "cold" strikes himself, a serious-minded man willing to do anything the navy expects of him, this presents problems in ethics only surmounted by the baffling confusion of the T.O of his command. For instance, how valuable could a seal be as a guided missile? Who's responsible when monkeys take over the running of a submarine?

Noted for the barbed satire of his science-fiction novels, Frederik Pohl is at his best in this acidly amusing, thoroughly preposterous, and unnervingly realistic novel of the future.

co-author of:

The Space Merchants

Search the Sky

Gladiator-at-Law

A Town Is Drowning

Presidential Year

editor of:

Star Science-Fiction Stories

SLAVE SHIP

by

Frederik Pohl

THE SCIENCE FICTION BOOK CLUB
by arrangement with
DENNIS DOBSON
London 1962

© FREDERIK POHL 1957

*This Science Fiction Book Club edition was produced in
1962 for sale to its members only by the proprietors,
Phoenix House Ltd. at 10–13 Bedford Street, London
W.C.2 and at Letchworth Garden City Herts. Full
details of membership may be obtained from our London
address. The book has been reprinted by A. Wheaton
& Co. Ltd., Exeter. It was first published by Dobson
Books Ltd.*

I

WE HAD a guided-missile scare on the flight down from Montauk, but it turned out to be one of our own. It came screaming in toward our line-of-flight, clearly visible through the windows of the transport plane, and you could hear a hundred and forty passengers taking a deep breath all at once. But its IFF radar recognized us. It veered off, spun around and went off hunting a Caodai—not that there were any around to find, as far as I knew.

So we landed right on schedule. And there I was on the coast of Florida. Hating it.

There wasn't any helicopter waiting. I arranged with the girl at the stationery stand—only a rating, but rather attractive—for the use of a phone, and called the number that was on my orders. A voice at the other end of the phone guessed, rather offhandedly, that they would get somebody down to meet me pretty soon; I claimed my baggage and sat back to wait for the helicopter.

The waiting room was crowded, and it was a long wait. I had been up all night, ferrying ashore from my cruiser at its station on the picket line, waiting for transport at Montauk, then the long flight down. I began to doze off.

Somebody shook my elbow.

"You'll have to move, Lieutenant." It was a stocky marine with a shore patrol armband. "Prisoners coming through."

"Oh . . . thank you." I got up and got out of the way. A transport had landed on the strip outside, and a file of short, wiry-looking Caodais was coming down the ramp, hands clasped atop their heads, armed SP guards covering them. I looked at them curiously. It was the first time I had seen the enemy in the flesh, and they didn't look much like the posters in the officers' heads at training camp. These looked a little too dark, I thought, to be from Indo-China proper. Perhaps from the satellite states in the Near East.

1

"How'd you like to come up against those babies in a fight?" said an Air Force captain standing by my side.

I looked at him. "I often have," I said, and went back to the telephone booth. I felt a little ashamed of myself snubbing him. Still, it was true enough—we had our share of engagements aboard *Spruance,* and these stateside heroes give me a pain.

Project Mako's operations room was surprised. "You mean they didn't pick you up, Lieutenant?" a man's voice demanded incredulously. "Hold on."

I held on, and after a while the voice returned. "Sorry, Lieutenant," it said breathlessly. "The pilot fouled up. Give him fifteen minutes."

The waiting room was jammed with prisoners now, maybe a hundred of them. They were a quiet lot, for prisoners. There was roughly one Tommy-gun-carrying SP for every three unarmed Caodais, but even so it gave me a creepy feeling to be so close to them. Even in action, the closest I had ever been to a living Caodai aboard *Spruance* was a thousand yards of hundred-fathom water.

The Air Force captain gave me an injured look from where he was gaping at the Caodais, so I walked in the other direction. It was the first time I had ever been in Florida, and from the observation deck of the airport I could see a skyline of palm trees and hibiscus, just as the travel booklets had promised, back in the days when there were travel booklets. Those were pretty remote days, I told myself—only three or four years ago, but I was a civilian then, and so was my wife. The whole country was civilian then, barring eight or ten million cadres. It was hard to remember——

There was confusion and shouting behind me. "Grab him! No, stand back, you idiots—give him a chance to breathe! He's hurt!" I turned and reached for the sidearm that I wasn't carrying—an automatic reaction, because my first thought was that the prisoners were making a break.

But it wasn't the prisoners.

It was my friend from the wild blue yonder, and he was staggering and screaming, clutching the collar of his Air Force tunic. A couple of Navy men were trying

2

to hold him but he didn't even know they were there. Whatever it was that was hurting him, it was hurting him very much.

I started to run toward him, me and everybody else in sight. But it was a little late. He yelled something hoarse and loud, and fell over against the yeoman by his side; and you had only to look at him slumping to the floor to know that he was dead.

I stood there for a moment, staring at him. He had a dreamer's face, a kid not more than twenty or so; but he would never reach twenty-one.

In a moment the field medics were there and they carried him into an office, and everybody in sight asked the man at his side: "What happened? What did he do?"

Nobody had any good answers. The loudest of the theories was that one of the Caodais had smuggled a gun in and pot-shot the captain; but the shore patrol was positive that that was impossible. Impossible, first, that they could have had guns; even more impossible that any of them could have leaned past the guards at the waiting room doors and fired without the guard noticing it.

The only people who might have had any information—the Navy yeoman who had been beside him, and the medical officer from the field—were closeted inside the office, and there was an SP guard outside the closed office door who obviously didn't know anything and wouldn't tell you if he did.

It was a pretty exciting introduction and it got even more exciting, in a way, a few moments later. There was a screeching siren outside and three Army officers wearing the Intelligence insignia came leaping up the steps two at a time. They disappeared into the closed office, and stayed there.

That disposed of the faint possibility that it had been a natural death. I thought it was peculiar that they should have got Intelligence there in such a hurry. But I didn't know quite how peculiar it was.

The helicopter from Project Mako finally picked me up. The pilot, a short old CPO, was only moderately apologetic: "I forgot," he said cheerfully. "Say, what's all the excitement?"

I told him, overlooking the fact that he was in sloppy uniform and seemed a little extra careful not to breathe on me. "Killed him, hey?" he said, impressed. "You don't say!"

But the copter looked shipshape enough, in its freshly painted Navy markings, and the Chief seemed to know what he was doing as he took off.

We aimed at one of the towering cumulo-nimbus down the shore, a mountain of a cloud—boiling puffs of whipped cream piled over one another, the frayed thunderhead anvil teetering at the top. The CPO pointed at it with his chin and said:

"Gonna have a storm, Lieutenant. We get one every afternoon about this time. But don't worry, Charley'll beat it in."

That time I caught a whiff of his breath. I had been pretty sure he had been either drinking or popping. The breath told me which; you could have put ice cubes in it and served it at a cocktail party.

It was unfortunate that the first rating I encountered from Mako was drunk on duty, or the next thing to it. One of the most difficult problems a junior officer faces is keeping to the right side of the thin borderline between an easy relationship with the enlisted men on one hand, and outright Asiatic lack of discipline on the other.

I didn't want to start out on my new base by putting a man on report. I let it go, with some doubt in my mind. But the new base was beginning to sound strange—"farm-hands"—and it seemed to me that I'd best get my bearings.

Anyway, drunk or sober, he was flying the helicopter well enough.

And he seemed a friendly type. He picked a battered pair of glasses off the floor and handed them to me. "Prison camp." He pointed below. "Take a look if you want to, Lieutenant."

They were good glasses, and we were only a few hundred feet up. I could see, very clearly, the scattered compounds inside the barbed wire, and the sentry towers

4

all around. There seemed to be something going on inside the compound. A procession of a sort, with paper dragons and enormous paper figures. I spotted a dragon with a man's head, a paper Oriental temple, easily eight feet high, and all sorts of Mardi gras trimmings.

"What's the celebration?" I asked. The Chief took a quick look through the glasses and returned them to me.

"Ah, who knows?" he said genially. "They go on like that a lot. Did you see old Victor Hugo?"

I stared. "Victor who?"

"Hugo. The paper dragon there, with Victor Hugo's head on it," he explained. "See it? Victor Hugo's one of their saints, like. Funny, isn't it, Lieutenant? The guards give them the cardboard to make those things; it keeps the Cow-dyes out of trouble, I guess."

Victor Hugo! I stared through the glasses, until the camp was out of sight. There they were—the enemy. The members of the religious cult that had stormed out of old Viet Nam and swept over most of three continents, and appeared to be about ready to take on a couple more.

The CPO leaned back and stared at the clouds. He was motionless for so long that I began to wonder if he was asleep. But at some unremarked sign below he heeled the stick over and said:

"Here's your new home, Lieutenant."

I stared over the sill of the window. A cluster of buildings and what seemed to be pasture lands, groves of palm trees and more pasture.

"It looks like a dairy farm," I offered.

"Right on the button, Lieutenant," he agreed. But he winked. "Kind of a peculiar dairy farm, though. You'll find out."

He cut the switch at the edge of a plowed field. There was no suggestion of securing the machine. We jumped out and left it, bags and all.

"Come on, Lieutenant," he said. "I think the commander's in the milk shed."

Milk shed! But that's what it was; I could see for myself. The Chief led the way toward a low, open-sided

5

building. My feet were ankle deep in black soil.

Three or four men in farmhand coveralls were putting a herd of cattle through a milking stall. My guide went up and spoke to one of them—a tall, rawboned redhead in ripped, soiled coveralls—while I looked around for the commander.

The redhead said, "Thanks, Charley. Take his bags to the BOQ."

He came toward me, mopping his face with a bandanna, and right at that point I got a considerable setback.

This hayseed cowhand, whose lantern jaw was a clear week behind a shave, wore pinned to the lapel of his dirty coveralls the gold leaf of a lieutenant commander in the U. N. Navy.

I said: "Lieutenant Logan Miller, sir. Reporting as ordered."

"Welcome aboard, Miller," he said, sticking out his hand. "I'm Commander Lineback."

Well, I did the best I could, lacking an OOD to report to, lacking colors to salute, lacking everything that made the colorful ritual of Navy reporting for duty.

I asked myself a lot of questions, in that milk shed, while I was waiting at Commander Lineback's request for him to finish what he was doing. When finally he was done, and he walked with me to his headquarters office, he said what the CPO had said on the copter: "This used to be a dairy farm, Miller, and to a considerable extent it still is. But you'll find it's an unusual one."

And he went on to explain the operation of the dairy farm—how they planted forage for the cattle between rows of a cash crop, told the cattle what to eat and what to leave alone, how the cattle were far from bright and often had to be told eight or ten times before they understood.

But, though I listened carefully, he never said what was unusual about that.

II

You HAVE to remember that I was fresh from the big-ship Navy in Caodai waters. *Spruance* was a 12,000 tonner, a heavy undersea cruiser with a complement of nine hundred officers and ratings, and you could shave in your reflection from its brightwork.

Project Mako was . . . a dairy farm. And I was an officer of the Line.

Take the way Lineback had said: "Glad to have you aboard." There wasn't anything wrong with the words, but he smiled, and it was the wrong kind of a smile. As though he was kidding the Navy.

In three years I had learned that you do not, repeat *do not*, kid the Navy. It isn't a matter of flag-waving patriotism or anything like that, it's just good sense. The Navy was doing a man-sized job with the Caodais; if it hadn't been for the Navy, nothing in the world would have stopped them from opening up a beachhead somewhere along the ˙coast of Guatemala, say, or Ecuador. They were used to jungles. Like the Japanese at Singapore, where the defending guns were firmly emplaced to face the only "possible" attack, the sea—and the Japs had struck from the blind land side and won—once the Cowdyes got a toehold anywhere in the Americas they would plow their way right up and down the hemisphere. The jungle wouldn't stop them, and by then it would be a little late for the fusion bombs.

But the Navy stopped them, by doing things the Navy way. And you don't kid an outfit that's doing the job for you.

Commander Lineback shoved me off on his exec, a full lieutenant named Kedrick. He was a pot-bellied little man, obviously over age in grade, but at least he seemed pretty Navy—in a harried, fuss-budget sort of way. He logged me in and complimented me on my arrival, and listened to my mild complaint about the helicopter pilot. "Forgot to pick you up, eh? And drinking on duty, eh?" He sighed. "Well, Miller, good men are hard to find." And he showed me to my quarters.

The BOQ at Project Mako was what once had been a third-rate beachfront vacation hotel. The walls were paper and the rooms were made for midgets, but the plumbing was crystal and chrome. There was a magnificent view of the ocean; I was admiring it when Kedrick said briskly: "Draw the curtains, man. It's getting dark!"

I looked at him incredulously. "Blackout?" I asked. With radar and infravision, visible light made no particular difference to hostile vessels.

"Blackout," he said firmly. "Don't ask me why; but it's orders, something to do with the Glotch, I guess. Maybe they think the Caodais are sending it over by frogman—*they* need regular light."

I said humbly, "Excuse me, Mr. Kedrick, but what is the Glotch?"

"Good lord, man, how would I know? All I know is, people drop down dead. They say it's a Caodai secret weapon, and they call it the Glotch—heaven knows why. Is this the first you've heard of it?"

I hesitated. There hadn't been anything like that on *Spruance*, not even scuttlebutt. But I told him about the Air Force captain at the airport. He nodded.

"Sounds like it. Now you know as much as anybody else." He was looking tense, even for him. "We haven't had it here—Mako's a small station. But it's happened right in Boca before. One of the guards at the stockade, a couple of weeks ago, and a transient before that." He shrugged. "Not my problem," he said, dismissing it. He turned and paused in the doorway of my quarters, looking like nothing so much as a bellboy waiting for his tip. He said:

"The commander won't have time to talk to you about your duties here for a while, Miller. Matter of fact, I won't either. You'll get briefed in the morning—as much as you'll *get* briefed, that is. Until then, you'll have to cool your heels."

8

"That's all right, sir. It'll give me a chance to look around the station."

"The devil it will, Miller!" he said sharply. "Everything on the project is classified Top Secret and Need-to-Know. You'll get the word, when the time comes, from the commander, not before." He scowled at me as though I were a suspected pacifist. "Meanwhile," he said, "you're restricted to the BOQ, the wardroom and the headquarters area. And make sure you stay there."

Orders were orders, so I stayed there. With nothing to do. Back on the cruiser there had been plenty to do. I was posted to *Spruance* as a computer officer, since I'd majored in cybernetics; but as long as I was in a forward area I wanted to fight. They were glad to accommodate me. There is almost always a place for a man who wants to fight in a war, even a cold one.

I don't know why they called it a cold war anyhow; it seemed hot enough on *Spruance*. While I was aboard we had three confirmed Caodai kills—two merchantmen and a little surface corvette. Of course, they weren't officially Caodais; officially, they were "unidentified vessels in interdicted area." But it was funny how the Caodai patrols never sank any "unidentified" Asian or African shipping, any more than the U.N. fleet bothered the American. I suppose that if either side had intercepted a European ship it would have been quite a problem for the commander—if there had been any European ships for anybody to intercept.

They called it a cold war. But fourteen million of our men were hotting it up over in Europe, against twenty or so million of theirs. Our land casualties were comparatively low—in the low millions that is.

And no state of war.

There was just this one little thing: Our troops were killing theirs all the way from the Pyrenees to the White Sea in local "police actions."

Well, it really wasn't a war, not in the old-fashioned sense. For one thing, it wasn't country against country, the way it used to be when things were simple: It was

9

confederation—the United Nations—against a Church Militant—the Caodais. They were a religion, not a nation; they happened to be a religion with troops and battlewagons and fusion bombs, but a religion all the same. And how can you declare war against a religion?

Our ambassadors still maintained an uneasy residence in Nguyen-Yat-Hugo's court. Every day or so the ambassador would show up at Yat's giant Cambodian temple with a fresh note of protest over some fresh killing; and the answer was always "Gee, sorry, but you'd better take that to the Iranian (or Pakistani or Saudi-Arabian or Viet Namese) authorities, not us." And diplomatic relations went limpingly on. And so did a certain amount of trade, so you could tell that it wasn't really a *war*.

But the best way to tell that it wasn't a war was that the fusion bombs stayed nicely tucked into their satellite launchers, theirs and ours. Silly? Not so very silly, no—the bombs were all too able to end the "war" overnight, by ending everything.

So everybody played the same game, we and the Caodais, because everybody had the same powerful desire to keep the fusion bombs right where they were. The rules were fairly simple: No landings in force on the enemy continents (but islands were fair game). No attacks on enemy shipping in "open" waters (but sink anyone you like in interdicted areas—and interdict any waters that suit your fancy). But it was never called "war."

For some people it was a pretty high-stakes game. Not so much for me, you understand: though *Spruance* had been in a forward area, we'd never come up against anything as big as we were. But it was a mighty rough police operation for the ones who saw water hammer in when the depth bomb connected, the ones who took a hunk of gelignite in the navel, the ones who lost a wing at thirty thousand feet and found the escape hatch buckled.

But not for me. Especially not at Project Mako.

The next morning I waited hopefully at breakfast for someone to tell me to report for briefing, but nobody did.

10

It was raining, and everybody else seemed to have work to do, so I picked some books out of the shelf in the wardroom—Mahan and Jellicoe—and talked the mess boy out of some coffee. It never hurts to refresh yourself on classical tactics.

Commander Lineback came slouching through the wardroom just before lunch while I was reading *The Grand Fleet*. He gave me a strange look.

"Glad to see you're improving your mind." he said. "Everything going all right?"

"Well, yes, sir," I said, "except——"

"The briefing's postponed till this afternoon," he said, and was gone.

I was being treated like an interloper. I told myself that COMINCH didn't think I was an interloper; COMINCH, from the majesty of his five stars, had picked me out of *Spruance* and crash-prioritied me to this hole in the Florida swamp. Maybe Lieutenant-Commander Lineback didn't have time to bother with me, but I was a skilled and talented naval officer and not constitutionally fitted for being a bum. I had thirty-five sweeps to my own credit—ranging up to a hundred miles from *Spruance* in my little battery-powered scout torp—and though I didn't have any kills, I had an official assist on the corvette; I'd flushed it right into *Spruance's* jaws.

After lunch everybody disappeared again, and I was tired of the wardroom. I put on my oilskins and wandered around the headquarters area, watching the big, warm drops smash the bougainvillaea blooms. It was kind of pretty, Florida was; I thought about maybe some day, my wife and I, coming here for a second honeymoon . . .

If I ever saw her again.

Maybe, I thought to myself urgently, walking a little faster, maybe if I put it to the commander right he'd let me go into town, and I could have a few drinks, perhaps even pop a couple.

But it wouldn't do any good. I'd tried drinking, and it didn't let me forget that my wife was a long, long way away. I kicked at the watery hibiscus morosely. It's tough

11

enough to go to war and leave the girls behind you. But what about when they don't stay behind you?

"Moo-oo."

I looked up, startled.

I had been thinking, not watching where I was going. I had wandered along a shell-bordered walk, past a truck garden the enlisted men kept on the side, into a grove of coconut palms. And on the other side of the palms was a shack, and in the shack a cow was monotonously lowing.

The question was, was I still in the headquarters area?

I looked around me. Nobody had told me exactly what the headquarters area was, I reminded myself defensively. It wasn't my fault if I was outside it.

The shack had one curious feature, considering that a cow was lowing inside it: It had only a regular human-sized door. There were windows, but I couldn't see through them. But I could hear, all right.

That cow sounded unhappy—sick, perhaps, or wanting to be milked, though it was the middle of the afternoon. "Moo-oo," it went, and then, in a lower key with a sort of grunt at the end: "Moo-oo-oo." Then the first one again, and the second, in an alternation too regular to be believed.

Well, what could be more natural than to hear cattle lowing on a dairy farm? But the regularity bothered me, and so did the door; I walked closer.

And the door opened in my face.

Lieutenant Kedrick was standing there, turned away, talking to a hawk-faced j.g. whom I had seen at lunch. The j.g. was gesturing with a spool of recording tape; he saw me over Kedrick's shoulder and his expression changed.

Kedrick turned around.

"Miller," he said.

I cleared my throat. "Aye-aye, sir," I said.

He stepped out into the rain, staring at me. He hardly noticed the drops splattering off his slicker, he was so angry. "Miller," he said, "curse it, you were restricted to the area! Now, get back to your quarters and wait for the briefing."

12

I said, "Sir, I——"

"*On the double, Mr. Miller!*"

I saluted. "Yes, sir."

But why? It wasn't as though there was anything in sight that justified all that security. I suppose that everyone is familiar with dairy farms, and that's about all there was to see on Project Mako. I'd already seen enough to last me a lifetime; I had spent part of my teens doing summer work in upstate New York, where you can't throw a rock between Albany and Syracuse without hitting somebody's Holstein.

Of course, southern cattle aren't Holsteins, but they all operate about the same. Those at Project Mako (once called the Volusia County Dairymen's Co-op Center) were divided into two herds, one purebred Santa Gertrudis, the other Brahman-Friesian crossbreds. But the husbandry was the same. The milk sheds were the same; the forage was the same; the cattle themselves lowed and ate the same and were milked the same.

Project Mako's number two crop happened to be hybrid teosinte, the Mexican bush corn. Back in Cayuga County we mostly used potatoes for the secondary crop, but it didn't matter: You plant your potatoes, or corn, or anything you like in rows; you show the cattle your specimens of the money crop in its various stages of growth; and you turn them loose. The cattle eat the weeds and leave the crop. Their droppings fertilize the pasture, and the "weeds" make milk for you. They tell me the old folks used to do the same thing with geese and cotton. But it was just luck that geese didn't like the taste of cotton stalks; with cows, speaking their language, you could *tell* them what to eat and what to leave alone.

They weren't really weeds, of course. You don't want your cattle eating real weeds; best practice in Cayuga County, where I came from, was to sow a cover crop of one of the ladino grasses or hybrid clover, something that would stand up under heavy grazing. Naturally you don't want it to look too much like your money crop, either, since cows are not bright.

13

But what was top secret about that?

I relied on the briefing to explain all these questions to me, but the briefing was a huge disappointment.

The new draft of officers arrived while I was wandering around the Project, over a dozen of them; and we all assembled in the wardroom at 1600 hours. There was a Russian, the usual batch of American junior officers, Commander Lineback, and a civilian.

The civilian did the actual briefing. His name was Schwende, and Commander Lineback referred to him as "Doctor." Well, the briefing didn't amount to much; all Schwende said was that we were going to do research in communicating with animals. Why? He didn't say why. How?

There would be a few new wrinkles. Dairy farmers, as I have mentioned, had given orders to their cattle for some time. But we were going beyond cows and horses and pigs, beyond the order to lay off the cash crop and the demand to return to the barn for milking. We were going to *talk* to them.

"You'll make guesses," said the doctor (of animal husbandry, not medicine). "That's your privilege. Guess your heads off about what the Navy's going to do with animals. *But keep your guesses to yourself.*"

And that was the end of that, barring the handing out of individual assignments. Mine was to run a computer.

We were dismissed, and the new draft of officers reported to the dayroom to be assigned to quarters. All of the new ones were ensigns and j.g.'s, except for the Russian. He was some kind of senior lieutenant, but just what that amounted to I cannot say. It didn't matter in terms of command relationship, of course, because as a co-belligerent he was present only as a military observer. He was a Red Army man, not Navy, but he wore our naval undress whites, with only the Russian shoulder-bars to mark his rank.

And he was quartered with me.

A room to myself had been too good to last. I showed him to our room with only minor regrets for the loss of

14

my solitude. In hesitant but good English he said: "Is very nice, Lieutenant. Which of the beds is yours?"

I offered him his choice, but he insisted on not disturbing my arrangements. "Both of them are splendid," he declared judiciously, and then he smiled. It was a good smile; with it he came to rigid attention. "Timiyazev, Semyon Ilyitch," he proclaimed. "Please to call me Semyon."

I helped him unpack, and we made ourselves acquainted. He knew more about Project Mako than I had before the briefing; but nothing that was very informative. He had been thoroughly briefed by his Government-in-exile at their tiny legation in Washington, just next to the dome of the United Nations building. He said, "They were very glad to be able to send me to this place. We have not so very many officers in the Free Russian Forces who are versed in animal psychology, do you see? Much less one who is the son of a colleague of Pavlov's."

"I didn't know it ran in the blood."

He looked at me appraisingly, then chuckled. "Oh, it does not. Surely not. But my mother was also my teacher. She was unhappy when my opportunity came to attend the Suvorov Academy. She would have preferred, you see, a scientific life for me. But in a world at war, one is best as a soldier. And if one must be a soldier, why not attend the Academy and have perhaps the prospect of becoming a general?" He added pensively, "That was some years ago, of course. Before the Orientals occupied us. Now—perhaps my mother knew best."

I made my excuses after a little while. Semyon made me just a little uncomfortable.

I know that the Russian business is all done and over, and you don't hold a grudge against somebody who's down. And, in a way, it's our fault that the Russians are in the kind of shape they're in. If we hadn't pulverized them so thoroughly in the Short War, they wouldn't have been so soft a touch ten years later for the Caodais coming over through Mongolia. And if they had been able to hold on for a while then, long enough for us to get off the

15

dime, the Caodais might have been stopped in their tracks right there, as Hitler might have been stopped at the Sudetenland. And universal conscription might not have been necessary, and my wife might not have been so many thousands of miles away . . .

And if wishes were horses, beggars would ride the winners at Tropical Park.

Howsoever, we got to work.

The next morning Chief Oswiak picked up the Russian and me and took us in the helicopter to our base of operations.

I said: "I didn't see those buildings when you flew me in."

"Sure you didn't, Lieutenant," the Chief agreed. "They wasn't any buildings there to see. The Seabees come in yesterday morning, and more fuss and commotion you never heard in your life. But they got them up." He brought the copter down gently between two of the new buildings. Three-story prefabs, they were, with the workmen still laying power lines around them. "Looks like we're getting busy, all right," said Oswiak. And it did.

Computer officer—that was I. That was what I had done aboard *Spruance*, and that was what I was going to be doing at Mako. A chunk of one floor in one of the prefabs was all mine. It was my first assignment to supervise the installation of my computers, already on hand and waiting to be hooked up. After that—after tha I wasn't very clear; but, as I say, it had something to do with talking to animals.

Well——

At any rate, the computers were plenty big and plenty good. The Seabees had already made a start. I pitched in, and the job was completed by bed time. The night shift came on to test connections as I left. I stopped by my new roommate's quarters to see if he wanted a lift back to the BOQ.

But he didn't; it was well on to midnight, but he was busy doing something with a collie.

16

From the door I heard a clicking sound, like one of those tin gadgets from childhood called crickets. I looked, and that was what it was—formed tin body, hardened, cupped tin plate fitted into it. "What's up?" I demanded. Semyon looked up angrily. "Hush, Logan!" he ordered severely. "New dog, I must finish this trial. Stay where you are!"

The dog looked at me pleadingly. It was clearly confused; its tongue was hanging, it was panting, its slightly raised foreleg was quivering. Semyon didn't say another word. We all waited and the dog got tired first.

It started toward me, looked at Semyon, hesitated, stopped. Semyon was as silent as old Stalin in his tomb. The dog turned tentatively to one side, and *click* went the cricket in Semyon's fingers. The dog walked slowly to a straight-backed chair. *Click.* The dog touched the chair with its nose; *click, click.*

Yes, I was puzzled. Semyon had called it a "trial"; but all he was doing was clicking his little cricket. He didn't say a word, he hardly moved.

The dog was as puzzled as I, which was some consolation. It stopped and looked at Semyon; Semyon, blue eyes serene under his pale brows, looked calmly back. The dog took a hesitant step away from the chair, and paused, waiting for a reaction. Silence. The dog whined worriedly, and returned to the chair. *Click* went Semyon's cricket. The dog placed its forepaws on the seat. *Click, click.* The dog leaped up into the seat and curled up, tail wagging madly. *Click, click, click;* and then Semyon, grinning broadly, said:

"Fine dog. Oh, excellent dog! You may come in now, please, Logan." He walked over to the dog, talking to it in Russian, and scratched enthusiastically behind its ears.

"What the devil is it?" I demanded. "Were you sending Morse code?"

"Exactly," he beamed. "Oh, not precisely the Morse, you understand. But a code. We were talking, the dog and I."

17

"Some Russian invention?"

He shrugged modestly. "Of course a Russian invention. My own mother invented it herself, you will find it described in Great Russian Encyclopedia. Of course," he added judiciously, "she was assisted in inventing it by a man named Skinner in America, who invented it also, some years earlier. But my mother invented it in *Russia*, you see."

"Tell me," I demanded. Semyon was delighted, of course, but he was far from clear. It was a way of communicating with animals, but the animals couldn't talk back. It was a way of getting a dog to do what you wished, but it wasn't training.

"Is it the same thing Lineback uses for cows?"

"No, no!" he said. "Radically different, Logan!"

"Different how?"

Semyon gave me a queer look. I could see he was wondering how anyone as stupid as I had been assigned to Project Mako, but he was too polite to say so. He said only: "You have heard the cattle language. It is only a matter of listening to the sounds the beasts make—we will dismiss, for the moment, the visual components. One discovers how one beast informs another that there is, shall we say, a patch of clover here or a stinging-nettle there. Once you have learned the, shall we call it, ox-tongue—" he peered coyly at me—"you say it back to the beast. You make the stinging-nettle bleat for danger and pain; you say it to the beast, and you show him, perhaps, a clump of marigolds. Then perhaps he does not eat the marigolds. Of course, he perhaps slips sometimes, for he is quite stupid. He may take a nibble to see for himself. Then you beat him, and make the stinging-nettle bleat again, and he learns. Oh, he learns, surely; it is a question of time and repetition." He frowned at me and said argumentatively: "Is *training*, you see? The language is only to expedite the training."

"I see. And what you are doing?"

"It is *language*." He smiled abruptly and charmingly. "But I admit, Logan, it is a very tiny language. One

18

word: 'Yes.' My dog here, Josip; if he does as I wish, I say 'yes' to him. If he does what I do not wish, I say nothing at all, and he understands 'no.' I snap this thing for yes; I do nothing for no. A very simple language, isn't it?"

"Too simple. How can it work?"

He shrugged. "See for yourself. What would you have Josip do?"

"Do?"

"So I said, *do*. Set a task for him, Logan. We shall see."

I hesitated, and he flared up: "You think it is no language, yes? I see. You think it is some kind of trick or game, like trained dog acts in the fair. But see for yourself, Logan; give me an order and I will translate. Would you perhaps care to have Josip sit in your lap? Push the door you left ajar closed with his nose? Fetch you a book from the shelf?"

I said awkwardly, "I've seen trained dogs do some astonishing things——"

"Not trained!" he almost screamed. "Is absolutely untrained, this dog! Except for only one hour this afternoon, when I taught him the language. Nothing else. Is not training, Logan, you must understand that!" He cast about the room agitatedly. "No discussion," he said peremptorily. "Look here, I choose a task. You see the cardboard cup on the floor? Once it had coffee in it; I drank the coffee; I forgot the cup. I shall require Josip to pick it up and put it in the wastebasket. Neatness is important, is it not? Even for a dog."

"I had a Scotty who carried newspapers——"

"Logan! I shall stand behind this folding screen, peeping at him with only my eyes. I shall say nothing, except in our tiny language. One word, remember! No, no—no discussion, only watch."

He huffed and went behind the screen, the dog watching him worriedly.

It was a sad little spectacle, in a way. My sympathies were all with the dog. He knew something was expected of him, but he clearly did not know what. There was

19

silence from Semyon behind the screen, then the dog took a tentative step toward Semyon. Silence still. The dog, forlorn, took a step away. *Click* from Semyon.

The dog brightened and, with assurance, took several more steps. *Click, click, click;* and then the clicking stopped. The dog had veered away from the direction of the paper cup.

Josip was beginning to get the hang of it. He lolled his tongue worriedly for only a second, then he tried another direction, at random. Silence. Then another, and this time it was straight for the cup. *Click, click* until the dog was standing right at the cup, touching it with his nose.

It might have taken three or four minutes in all, but, guided by Semyon's cricket noises, the dog unarguably did exactly what Semyon had promised. He pushed the cup, touched it with his paw, rolled it with his nose. Eventually he picked it up, and eventually he carried it to the wastebasket. Like Shannon's mechanical mouse, he made random motions until he found one that paid off (with a *click*); and continued with it purposefully until the pay-off stopped.

It all went quite rapidly. The cup went into the wastebasket and Semyon came gleefully from behind the screen. "Ah, Logan?" he asked. "Training? Or language?"

I was getting sleepy. I left him and looked in on the last stages of checking my digital computers.

Well, I am no more stupid than most; but man's mind is divided into compartments, leakproof and thought-tight. I had been polite with Semyon, but I had not been convinced.

Set aside the question of what it all had to do with the Navy or the Caodais—that was a separate problem. On its own merits, what Semyon was doing was interesting enough. And perhaps it was even important, in a way. But to call it language? Ridiculous. I had at least a nodding acquaintance with the theory of language. Language is a supple and evocative thing; how could you dignify a one-word vocabulary by that term? Imagine compressing information, any quantity whatsoever of information into a simple yes-and-no code.

Thinking which, I checked the installation of my digital computers, capable of infinite subtle operations, packed with countless bits of knowledge and instruction. And all of it transcribed, summarized and digested into what the mathematicians call the binary system, and reproduced in the computers by the off-or-on status of electronic cells.

III

MAYBE I WAS STUPID. But you have to admit that the idea of binary language is hard to take.

Animals, after all, are not electronic computers. They are flesh and blood like ourselves. I would have thought of talking to animals in a mathematical code about as soon as I would have thought of talking to my RAGNAROK in German. . . .

And then I found out that, way back in the fifties, people had begun to do just that. I poked through the briefing documents in the project library until I found a resume of some trials that had taken place, long ago, in England, on a computer called APEXC—heaven knows why. They set the computer the problem of translating German into English; and the computer, no doubt, clicked and hummed and blew a couple of fuses, and then settled down to the job of squeezing the sense of one language into the forms of another.

It didn't say just how well APEXC made out, but there were hints. In the first place, some mere human had to give APEXC a hand in the clinches—what they called post-editing, meaning the choice, from context, of several possible translations for a single word. But it worked.

So I read farther—on animal communication, this time. I found Semyon's mother's "invention" in the literature— also way back in the early fifties. I found sample vocabularies for cow, for dog, for crow, even for rabbit and duck. Some of the "words" were kind of interesting. For crow, a B-natural whole note, two staccato A-sharp quarter notes and a scattering of grace notes. Translation: Beat it, there's an eagle coming. Crow was one of the simpler vocabularies, only about fifty identified words; but it was astonishing what *corvus* could convey to his friends with a few simple caws. And some of the beasts, nearly mute, got considerable meaning across without any sound at all.

22

Take the Bombay duck's train-switching wiggle of the tail feathers, for instance. Translation: "I love you very much, honey, let's get married."

I suspected, at about that point, that some of the early researchers were carried away by their senses of humor. "Language?" I complained to Semyon in our quarters, while I was reading the briefing books and he was playing something he called a balalaika, "How can they call that language? If my mouth waters, that means I want to eat, but is mouth-watering a word? It's only a reflex action, Semyon!"

He didn't miss a chord. He fired at me: "Is better, Logan, that you consider the analogy of onomatopoeia!"

Well, that stopped me—until I looked it up; and then it stopped me in a different way. Onomatopoeia: the formation of words from instinctive or mimetic sounds, thought by some to be the essential origin of all language.

All right, grant Semyon's point. Assume that the supple English language was really nothing but a refined and codified collection of yelps and wheezes. Assume that animal grunts and posturings were language as well.

What did all that have to do with me?

Finding out took some time—and a lot of work, of which my own was about the smallest part. Remember Manhattan Project? It had a big, difficult, important job. The United States needed an isotope of radium—U^{235}, as every schoolboy knows—and they needed lots of it. They even knew ways they might get it—had already got it, in fact, in microgram quantities. There was thermal diffusion—the endless flow of uranium salts through osmotic barriers. There was the mass spectrograph. There was the "breeder" reaction; and there were others. Manhattan Project had to make a decision.

So they decided to do them all.

That was the military mind at work, and who is to say they were wrong? Project Mako worked along the same lines. We had half a dozen paralleling projects going at once. Lineback's own group was tediously expanding their vocabulary of Cow. Semyon Timiyazev was bedeviling his little dogs with yes-no codes, persuading *them* to talk to *him*. A team of four full lieutenants was reading meaning into the elevation of a dog's tail, and translating it into flipper-positions for the seals they were given to work with. And more.

And I, with a fifty-year-old WAVE, a Barnard graduate with a degree in statistical mathematics, to help me, was assigned the programming of a computer series that would make sense out of what they were doing.

It wasn't easy. It was simple enough to assign conceptual values to the parts of language, and I couldn't complain about the equipment the Navy gave me. The basic unit was an old mercury-delay RAGNAROK; but some considerate genius in BuSup had added a self-checking circuit to flush triple voltage through the tubes to pick off the bad ones, between operations; so that the unit was pretty reliably good for 99-six-nines per cent effective operation. There were forty-eight memory tanks in the mercury-delay class, plus a batch of magnetic drums for instructions and a large electrostatic storage unit. With its card punch, reader and teleprinter, it pretty well filled my space. I looked at it and felt something like the midget who married the fat lady: It was a lot of computer to handle all by myself.

But the hard part wasn't running the computer, it was making sense out of what came out.

Semyon had told me so. He formed the habit of dropping in on me for a coffee break now and then. More now than then; I don't know if all Russians are the same way, and if they are it might account for the way they made out in the war, but he seemed to need his coffee break every hour on the hour. He said:

"Is a question of vocabulary, Logan. RAGNAROK has not the vocabulary."

I said stiffly, "A computer a quarter the size of RAGNAROK translated Russian back in the fifties."

"Ah, Russian, you say," he said mildly. "It is the language of animals, you say?"

"Oh, Semyon. I didn't mean——"

"No, no, no, I do not mean I am insulted. I only ask, is Russian the language of animals? It is not, we will suppose. It is merely a human language."

"Merely?"

"Merely! Small vocabulary, you see. Not like animal, *large*."

I stared at him. "If I understand what you're saying," I said, "which is unlikely, you're trying to tell me that animals have a bigger vocabulary than Russ—than people."

"Exactly so, Logan." He nodded gravely. "Think! Is it engraved on your machine, that motto? 'Think.' Read the motto, Logan, and do as it says. Think, for example, if an animal possesses the capacity for abstract thought. He does not, you will say? Correct."

"But—that makes a smaller vocabulary, doesn't it?"

"Ah." Semyon crossed his legs, sipped his coffee and got ready for a nice, long chat. He said professorially: "Be, for the moment, my little dog Josip, and think of how he thinks. Are you and I 'men', Logan, in Josip's eyes? Or is each of us *a* man, an individual—you, perhaps, 'man who sits and watches' and I 'man who makes clicking sounds and gives food'? It is the latter, you will see. For that is how nouns begin in speech, as proper nouns, not class-words but names for particular things. This is why, with Josip, I have followed in the great tradition of my mother and cut to the root. Two words! Just a single word and a silence which is——"

"You told me," I said shortly. "Do you mean that to an animal each *thing* has its own individual word?"

"I simplify," Semyon said sunnily. "But you grasp my meaning."

I did; and I also grasped his arm and escorted him to the door. But it made the job look even harder than before.

But things got done. Almost without knowing it, we were in full swing. The seeker groups fed me long lines of symbols, representing, they thought, the conceptual elements of the language of cows and seals, dogs and rabbits, cats and pigs. We got nowhere with the rabbits—too stupid; and the pigs were farm bred, too fat to do anything but eat. But with the other animals there was progress.

The seekers watched the animals as Harun-al-Rashid did his harem favorites. They recorded every sound, photographed every movement. With chemical nostrils they examined the odors the animals gave off (someone had remembered that bees use odor to indicate sources of nectar); with a million dollars' worth of electronic equipment they palped the electromagnetic spectrum for signals that coarse human senses could not read.

And they found things. Sound, scent, body posture, bodily functions: These were the elements of language.

To whatever seemed to have meaning they assigned a symbol—even if the meaning itself was not clear. (Usually it wasn't.) Then they had a list of the essential parts of the animal vocabulary—lacking translations for the most part, but very nearly complete. And that was half their job.

And the other half was to record, in infinite detail, everything the animals felt and saw and experienced: That was the list of referents for the "word" symbols.

The two lists gave, first, the "words," second, the meanings.

And then it was up to me and my WAVE to tape them, program them, and feed them to RAGNAROK, so that RAGNAROK's patient electronic mind could, from frequency and from context and from comparison with the known parts of other languages, match symbols with referents, and make for us a dictionary of Pig and Cat and Seal.

I made the dictionary; but when I thought I could use it to win an argument with Semyon, I was out of my mind. He came wandering in one afternoon for coffee and found the first pages of a typed report summarizing what we had learned of Essential Cat.

I tapped him on the shoulder. "It says 'Most Secret' at the top of the page," I reminded him.

26

"Eh?" He looked at me absently. "Of course, Logan. Most interesting. I will return it in the morning."

I stopped him as he was walking out the door and took it away from him. I said gently, "You'll probably get a copy, but not from me. Anyway, you won't enjoy it, because it makes a liar out of you."

"Oh?" He twinkled at me. "Is difficult, Logan. How often can a maiden be betrayed? And what is this lie?"

I hesitated, then showed him—after all, he'd already looked at it. "Cat," I said. "Look them over, Semyon. Fifty-eight symbols, that's all. Seven tail movements, three kinds of rictus, twenty-two noises—add them up. Fifty-eight; and you said the animal vocabulary would be larger than the human."

"I did," he acknowledged. "And I still do. Fifty-eight symbols, but are they fifty-eight words? I think not. Call them phonemes, like the sounds of English. There are forty-some of those, I think? But put them together this way and that, and you have three, four, I do not know how many hundred thousand words." He sighed. "Do you see?"

Oh, I saw. But I didn't believe him. But if Semyon hadn't convinced me with all of his logic, he had still accomplished something, for he got me interested in the work we were doing.

Consider the jackdaw. Browsing among the reference materials in our library, while my overworked WAVE programmed like a mad thing, I found that there was a man named Konrad Lorenz who managed to talk Jackdaw back when Hitler ruled Germany. That was interesting. I hadn't thought of birds talking—the sailor's parrot, yes; but "parroting" had become a symbol of empty and uncomprehending making of sounds, and it was rather a surprise to find that Lorenz had managed to speak to jackdaws, to understand their mating terms and their rattling "Hey, rube!" warning call. Lorenz had learned how to call a greylag goose to him: "Rangangang-ang, rangangangang." And the same term in Mallard was: "Quahg, gegegegeg; quahg, gegegegeg!"

27

I learned how to say "hello" in Chimpanzee, a sort of coughing "Oo-oo-oo!" And at last I learned what Semyon was talking about, when I discovered how the beaver's slapped tail on the water is colored by context, how the white-tail deer's lifted "flag" can signal either alarm or all-clear.

But all the same, when he came in and found me in our room, surrounded with ancient texts, I told him: "You're wrong. The animal vocabularies are smaller than ours. They make one word do the work of many—but so do we."

He sighed. "*Khorashaw*," he said. "That is to say, all right, never mind, I agree with you. It is the Russian for 'okay.' Have it your way. It is an argument. you must understand, which can be won by either side, and I do not wish to pursue it further."

Because he'd lost, of course. It was disappointing to have him give in so easily. I suppose I looked a little irritated, because he said anxiously: "You are not angry, Logan? It is a foolish argument if it angers friends. We shall not be angry, shall we?"

I looked at him, as friendly and as wistful as his own little dog, and there was only one answer.

I glanced at the book in my lap and I said: "Hok hug-hug, hag kuag, guaggak."

He stared at me.

"That," I explained, "is Gibbon for *Khorashaw*."

IV

It was black night. The stars were bright outside our window; and the Project Mako alarm bell was ringing General Quarters.

Semyon snored, sputtered, choked and sat up. I jumped out of my own bed, slammed down the shades, slapped on the light. It was the first GQ I had heard since I left *Spruance*, but the old habits didn't die. General Quarters meant get to your combat stations *now*. I was in my pants and on my way out the door before the springs on my bed stopped vibrating, and Semyon was only a yard behind me. The only thing was, *what* combat stations?

But we did what came naturally, and I suppose it was the right thing to do. We found ourselves out in the corridor, along with every other officer in the BOQ. Semyon, buttoning his shirt, bawled over the noise: "What is, Logan? Can it be that the Orientals have attacked?"

There was a rattle from the loud-hailer before I could answer, and Kedrick's tinny voice came over it, blaring: "All officers to the wardroom, on the double! All officers to the wardroom! On the double!"

We swept into the wardroom like the Golden Horde through Russia—and just about as unkempt. The mess attendants showed up, blinking and rubbing their eyes; Kedrick, standing on a table with a strange Army major next to him, snapped: "Coffee, you men! On the double! We're pulling out of here in twenty minutes."

As the mess attendants were disappearing, Kedrick shrilled: "Shut up, everybody! Keep it down! The Cowdyes are busting out of the stockade and we're going to shove 'em back in. Major Lansing will explain."

The exec bobbed his plump chin at the strange Army officer, who growled: "Now you know as much as I do, except for details. I'm security officer at Eighth Group, up the beach; about an hour ago there was some ship-to-shore shelling, mostly flares and noisemakers; and then the damn

29

Cow-dyes began boiling up. They swamped the guards, took our headquarters building, knocked out our radio, and kept on going. I've got six personnel-carrying copters outside——" I recognized then the fluttering rumble that had been subconsciously bothering me "——and you're the nearest effectives." He glanced at us wryly, but let it go at that. "Your commander is already on his way there; Lieutenant Kedrick and I will command two columns to relieve the guards. If there are any guards left to relieve by the time we get there." He moved aside as the mess men came in with the first pots of coffee. "I'm sorry," he added, "to be going out of channels this way, but war is hell." He glanced at his watch. "We're taking off in five minutes. You want coffee, drink it. You want more clothes, go get them. Weapons will be issued at the copters."

And that was that. It was like being in the Navy again.

Semyon, sleepy-eyed and wobbly, shouldered his way to me. "Ah, Logan!" he exulted. "We shoot some Orientals, I imagine. It will give me pleasure. Only"—he looked oddly shy—"a favor, Logan?"

I burned my lips on the coffee. I managed to say, "What favor?"

"Josip. Fortune knows what your Bureau of Supply will do with him if I do not return; I do not suppose that a dog is a standard article to be furnished to ships and shore installations. Will you——"

I stared at him. "Sure," I said weakly.

It was just cracking daylight as we came fluttering down into the mangroves. There was no sign of the ship-to-shore firing the major had talked about, but out over the pearl-skied Atlantic I could see the lights of hunter copters stabbing at the waves; if there were Caodai vessels out there, they would be wisest not to surface. It would be a while before marine vessels with any range could reach the scene; but the copters were there, and I imagined I could see the skittering hydrofoils on the surface.

"Ssst!" said Semyon sharply as we banked and dipped.

30

"Over there, Logan! Like beetles in barn dung!"

"What? What?" I was a little jumpy, I suppose.

"The Orientals," gloated Semyon. And then, with an abrupt change of pace, utter dejection: "The fools, the fools, the fools! Why do we not hit them from above, eh? Bomb them, shoot them——"

"They're prisoners, Semyon!" I said, shocked.

"A prisoner escaped is scarcely a prisoner, my friend. What is better, to shoot them from above, where they can scarcely do us much harm? Or to sic in the bushes below, and wait for them to come?"

I said uneasily, "The major looks like he knows what he's doing, Semyon." He shrugged a large Russian shrug; and that was all he said. But he carefully checked the clips on his T-gun.

The copters came down in a clearing, and the major jumped on a stump to disperse us. "They're moving slow," he bellowed, "but they're moving. Soon as you see anything, shoot it! They've got some guns, captured from the guards; dunno how many or whether this lot has them. There's upwards of five thousand of them running around, so you'll have plenty of targets. Miller!"

I jumped. Of all the things I might have expected, being called out by name just then wasn't one of them. "Front and center, Miller," bawled the major. "The rest of you disperse and take cover."

But it had an explanation. I saluted the major with more snap than I'd been able to put into a salute for weeks. He clipped: "Miller? You the one that's checked out on a scout torp?"

"Checked out!" I started to blaze; but this wasn't the time for it. I said only, briskly: "Better than eight hundred hours in combat sweeps, with a confirmed——"

"Sure," he said, unimpressed and unheeding. He jerked a thumb and I found myself trudging through the mangrove swamp with a female naval ensign, toward the shore.

We looked at three scout torps lashed to a Churchill dock, bobbing harmlessly in the gentle morning swell.

31

She said bitterly: "Half our complement on leave—understaffed to begin with—the filthy swine!" She didn't make clear whether the "swine" were COMCARIB or the Caodais; but it was perfectly clear that she, as temporary exec officer while the male strength of the torpedo-squadron complement was manning the other torps, was requesting me to take one of the idle scouts out on a sweep.

She didn't have to ask me twice.

I slid out on the surface, and two hundred yards from shore checked the sealer telltales, flooded the negative buoyancy tanks and tipped the diving vanes. I leveled off at thirty meters—plenty deep for the continental shelf.

My search pattern was clipped to the board over my scanning port. I flexed the vanes a couple of times to get the feel of the torp; it was good to be home again. All these scouts come off the same assembly lines and are made out of the same interchangeable parts; but it is astonishing how much the "feel" can differ between craft. I set the auto-pilot for the first leg of the sweep; triggered the sonars; and I was off.

Back to *Spruance!* I felt like a fighting man. And there was, in truth, some chance that I might see some action. The girl ensign had filled me in a little bit on the way down to the beach; there really had been ship-to-shore firing—guided aerial torpedoes, mostly—and that meant at least a few Caodai vessels somewhere within range. Of course, "range" was anything up to 12,000 miles, and the only reason it wasn't more is that you can't get more than 12,000 miles away from anywhere and still be on the earth. But she thought, though she wasn't clear why, that they were pretty close inshore.

It was an exciting prospect. I tasted the implications of it, thoughtfully. Both sides in the cold war were being pretty meticulous about respecting the continental masses belonging to the other side. You couldn't say as much for islands, and naturally Europe was respected by no one at all, being a selected jousting field. But even guided-missile attack was very rare. I wondered what on the Florida coast made the Caodais mad enough to shoot.

32

The blow-off, of course, would be if they attempted a landing.

I remembered what Kedrick had said about expecting trouble from the stockade; the girl had talked as if everyone knew the prisoners were seething for weeks past. How the devil, I demanded of myself, could you be expected to know what was going on when security kept everybody's mouth shut? Was it fair to drag me out of bed when——

Two things stopped that train of thought. One was the faintly shamefaced realization that I was loving every minute of it. The second was the sonar sighting bell loud in my ear. I read the telltales fast: It wasn't a whale or a clump of weed. The microphones had picked up another sonar. And the IFF filters had spotted it instantly as an enemy.

I hit the TBS button—and prayed there was someone within range to hear: "Unidentified object, presumed Caodai, sighted at Grid Eight Eighty-Baker-Forty-Two." I read my co-ordinates off the autolog. "Object bearing fifty-five degrees from present position, range extreme, size unknown." That was it. *If* the sonar communicator got as far as someone who could hear—and *if* the understaffed, overworked squadron complement could spare a pair of ears to listen—then I might get reinforcements, possibly even in time to help.

Until then it was up to me.

I fed the coal to the screws and came about, tripping the safeties on the bow tubes. I had four tiny homing missiles to squander; any one of them, small as they were, would probably do the trick if they connected with anything smaller than a cruiser. And they would do their best to connect: Their seeker fuses could tune in on the sound of the enemy screws, the temperature of the enemy hull, the magnetic deflection of the enemy steel, all at once; and if one bearing differed from the other two, they would reject that one. They would do their best; but of course the Caodais would be doing theirs. Their noise-makers would be clattering up the water at acoustic-focal

33

points hundreds of yards away; their "curtain" ports would be dropping thermal flares; their counter-magnet generators would be generating and killing magnetic fields stem and stern by unpredictable turns.

Still—I had four missiles. One would be enough.

I was closing in on them at maximum speed; trying hard to read the indications in the sonar. A little bright pip of light doesn't tell you much, but it got bigger and brighter, and it began to look like something a lot bigger than me.

All of a sudden I was thinking of Elsie, fantastic thoughts: Suppose this Caodai, whatever he was, hit me; and suppose I got free and swam to the surface; and suppose they picked me up as a prisoner; and suppose they interned me; and suppose, just suppose, that I wound up on Zanzibar. . . .

But then I had no time for fantasies. The big, bright splotch in the sonar plate shimmered and spattered into a cluster of dots. For a moment they wavered and tried to converge again—but it was a cluster, all right.

One, two, three . . . I counted, and counted again. But the count didn't make much difference.

I had four missiles, all right, but there were at least eight of them. They were corvettes at the least, by the size of them in the sonar screen. And I was a little thirty-foot torp, with four missiles to fight with. If I got a 4.0 hit with every one of them, that left only four to beat the dubbing out of me.

What is a hero? I didn't feel heroic; I felt scared. But I didn't turn around and run for it either.

They not only had the legs of me, they had the reach of me too. If I ran, they could catch me. If I attacked, they could pound me to pieces before I got within range. If I sat still and prayed, I would at least enhance my dubious prospects of getting to heaven, which would at any rate be something constructive so my last minutes on earth wouldn't be a total loss. But what I did was fight. It was habit and instinct and routine. Full speed forward, turn the navigation over to the auto-pilot. Cut the fire-control remotes in on missile Number One, discriminate, lock, arm, and fire. Cut in on Number Two, fire Number

Two. Cut in on Number Three, fire Number Three. Cut in on Number Four, fire Number Four . . . and *then* it was time to cut and run.

In fact, it was past time. They were on course for me and I was on course for them; we had closed to less than five thousand yards. By the time I came about, it was forty-five hundred; and a corvette can catch a scout torp with a forty-five hundred yard lead in roughly twenty minutes. It is only a matter of relative speeds. Of course, in twenty minutes I could be closer inshore than they would dare to follow.

But they didn't really have to catch me, you see. Their missiles would do the job for them.

I watched the sonar screen with very close attention—it was all I had to do. There were the eight of them, big and ugly by now; there were the four staggered little streaks that were my missiles. And there—yes, there, just before the lead Caodai, were two other little glowing streaks. They weren't mine. They were missiles, but they weren't mine.

I kicked the auto-armor pedal home. My scout was now defensively armed; it was dropping random-sized masses of fine-spun metallic wool into the slipstream, hoping to divert the Caodai missiles. Unfortunately they were doing the same; I saw a mushrooming flare around one of my missiles as it went off, far out of effective range of the enemy craft, triggered no doubt by just such a blob of chaff. And another; and then the sonar screen was awash with light from rim to rim; the pressure-spheres surrounding the exploding missiles confused the sound waves, made them return conflicting images. I scrambled the sonar screen and snapped on the audic; at least I would know if something big was getting close to me.

Something big was! But not the Caodais—it came from due south, down the coast, and it was big and fast. IFF gave the answer: It was a *Spruance*-class cruiser, coming to the rescue.

They might get me, but Big Brother was going to get

35

them! I snapped open the TBS and yelled excitedly, "Welcome to the party! I'll give you my bearings for cross-check. My grid position——"

But I didn't finish. Audic tinkled and cut out in my earphones; there had been a big, near-by explosion and the filters, designed to keep the wearer from ruptured eardrums, had cut off the amplification. I waited for the smash.

I never heard it, but I felt it. Something hit the side of my head; and that was all, brother, that was all. . . .

But——

"Only the good die young," growled somebody with a Russian accent.

I sat up abruptly. "Semyon!" I said. "What——?"

The heel of his hand caught me in the chest, and I went back down again. "Doctor says to lie still!" he scolded. "You should have been dead, Logan! Don't provoke fortune!"

Well, I was alive, though it took me a while to believe it. What had hit me had been nothing but concussion, and the torp, though sprung a little at the seams, was still intact. The auto-pilot cut itself off when the hull was breached and, when nobody took the controls, automatically surfaced the vessel—and hydrofoils found it, with me inside. But I was alive.

"Did they get them?" I demanded.

"Get who? The Orientals?" Semyon shrugged. "They did not yet have the courtesy to report to me, Logan. I can only assume——"

"All right. What about the stockade?"

"Ha," he said, sitting up. "Such a struggle, Logan. Through the jungle like savages, screaming and fighting, deadly beyond——"

"*What about the stockade?*"

He pouted. "Is over," he grumbled. "We fought a little bit, and then armor began coming up from the highway, and when the Orientals saw the tanks they ran. Oh, some got through; they will be caught."

36

So that was that. Well, I thought, leaning back against the pillows of the sick bay and listening to the thumping in my head, it wasn't so bad after all. A free ride in a scout torp—I'd thought I'd never get to pilot one again. A successful, or anyway fairly successful, combat sweep against superior odds. A sure commendation in my file jacket, maybe even a citation from COMINCH. Who knows, possibly a Navy Cross—stranger things had happened. And the whole thing was over, a pleasant interlude in a dull existence.

What I didn't know was that nothing is ever really over.

Semyon said commandingly: "The doctor." I sat up, and he pushed me down again.

The doctor poked me and looked into my eyes and said: "Back on duty in the morning. Meanwhile——"

He reached for a needle. I protested, "But, doctor, I can go to sleep without that!"

"That's good," he said, squeezing the plunger. It worked fast; I saw him going out the door, and then, magically, he was turning around and coming back, only it wasn't the doctor any more. It was Elsie, just the way she had been the day we were married, lovely and desirable and all the wife a man could want. "Darling," I said to her, and she said many things to me. She bent and kissed me, and held me in her arms; and then all of a sudden her left eye blossomed out in a ripple of greenish light, and then her nose; and then she was awash from side to side with light,' just like a sonar scope; and the rest of the dream was hardly pleasant at all.

V

THE CAODAI OUTBREAK was contained, and by the next morning I was feeling fine.

It was a taste of action and I welcomed it. I wasn't alone. Half the officers at Project Mako seemed to feel the way I had felt. They were Line officers, fighting officers; they hadn't asked to come here and didn't want to stay, and a touch of combat cheered all of us up. Even Lieutenant Kedrick, that cheerless old maid, gave me the morning off to convalesce—from the doctor's needle, not from my brush with Caodais—and he came in to see me, and actually smiled. "You've got a commendation coming, Miller," he said. "Maybe more."

"Thanks. What happened?"

"Oh——" He shrugged. "Who knows how the Cowdyes run these things? I guess they thought they could catch us off guard and liberate a few prisoners. Isn't the first time, Miller."

"Oh? I thought the mainland had never been touched."

"Hah." He slapped at the paper I had been looking at, his face wrathful. "What do you call that?"

I glanced at the paper; the headline said:

UMP July Draft Call Put at 800,000;
Manicurists, Bakers, Morticians Called

I didn't quite see the relevance. I said: "Well, it *is* full mobilization, of course——"

"I'm not talking about the draft! They got Winkler."

Winkler? I glanced again and saw the story.

General Sir Allardis Winkler, Military Attaché of the United Kingdom Government-in-exile, died at his home in Takoma Park, Maryland, last night of undetermined causes. General Winkler's body was discovered by a member of his family when——

38

I looked at Kedrick wonderingly. "Was General Winkler a friend of yours?"

"Man," he said severely, "don't you know what that is? Where've you been? It's the Glotch again. They got Winkler, just the way they got Senator Irvine last spring. Who's next, eh? That's what I want to know. Those damn Cow-dyes can pick us off, one by one, and we don't know dirt from dandruff how to stop them."

I said, "Ah, Lieutenant. It doesn't say anything here about any Glotch."

"Sure it doesn't! Expect them to print *that?* Can't you tell when they're covering up?"

I said humbly: "I've been out of touch, I guess."

"Um." He looked at me. "Oh—yes. Sea duty. You might not have heard on sea duty. They don't have the Glotch much under water."

"Not on *Spruance*, anyway."

He nodded. "You're lucky. I bet if there's been one, there've been fifty pieces like that in the paper in the last six months. General Winkler dies of undetermined causes. Senator Irvine found dead in bed. District Mobilization Director Grossinger dead of 'stroke.' Stroke! Sure, the Cow-dyes struck him dead, that's what kind of 'stroke.' Knocks them over, screaming and burning. And not just big shots, but all kinds of people. Why——"

Something was coming through to me, something that seemed familiar. I interrupted, "Lieutenant, I saw an Air Force captain a couple days ago that——"

"Why, I bet there's *thousands* killed that we don't even hear about! There was a guard at the stockade three, four months ago. Nothing about him in the paper of course, but it was the Glotch all right. And the deputy mayor of Boca, they said it was a heart attack but——"

"I wonder if this Air Force captain——"

"——it was the Glotch, all right. They don't tell us about it, that's all. Why? Because they don't know what to do about it. The big brass is scared witless. They're trying everything. They're trying blackouts, they're trying this, they're trying that. But they aren't getting anywhere, and

39

they're going to have to face up to it by and by, and then, my God, you're going to see panic, Miller! Because they can get us with the Glotch. This raid on the stockade, that was nothing; the Glotch can strike a thousand miles inland, it can kill anybody. Sooner or later they'll use it in big doses—maybe a whole city at a time, eh? And then what? You remember what I said, Miller . . ."

The stewards appeared. "Chow, gentlemen." And that was the end of that, and I never did get to tell Kedrick about the Air Force captain I had seen stricken down with my own two eyes.

But I had a lot to think about.

Semyon showed up for lunch, punctual as always. We chatted over the stockade break and our skirmish, and I tried to find out what he knew about the Glotch; but all he knew was the word. That didn't stop him from discussing it, though. By the time we got to dessert and coffee I was sick of the subject, and looking forward to getting back to work. I counted the spoons of sugar he dumped into his coffee: Six of them.

"Ah," he said, tasting the first sip, "one lives again. At the Academy was like heaven to drink coffee, Logan. Only once a day. And coffee was from Turkey, you know. Once——"

"Better drink it fast," I advised. "I have to get to work."

"——once four cooks drank coffee and died," he went on. "Whole batch had to be thrown away, because someone had put strychnine in it. Terrible." He frowned reminiscently. "Turk? One imagines so. Was terrible time——"

"Good-by, Semyon." I stood up.

"——was terrible time, when Soviets of Russia were surrounded by hostile nations. Now, of course," he shrugged, "it is greatly different. We are friend to all, what of us the Orientals left. Do you find this a lesson to you, Logan?"

He winked amiably at me, and I couldn't help smiling. It was hard to realize that his country and mine had torn each other apart for the salvage of the splinters not much over a decade before, when Semyon was a fresh eighteen-year-old junior officer, straight out of the Academy into the Yugoslav Push that had touched off the Short War. That was Semyon's first battle—against Marshal Tito's stubborn little army.

And now he had named his dog in honor of his late enemy, the marshal, whose real name was Josip Broz.

He was a nuisance, but it was with a little disappointment that I realized, later on, that he hadn't shown up for his three o'clock coffee break. And he didn't show up at four, and he was late, actually *late*, for dinner.

"Oh, Logan," he explained sorrowfully, staring without appetite at the plate the mess attendant put before him. "Josip is sick. Could someone have hurt him, Logan? He is bleeding, and he will not let me come near. Poor little dog, perhaps he has been in a fight. Bloody. And he behaves oddly. I play with him and show him tricks, and he whines and hides under the desk and whines again." He began to chew.

"Maybe you ought to call a vet."

"I did! Of course I did. And they said, 'Terribly sorry, old man, but it will have to wait; we must scrub the cattles' teeth for Commander Lineback first.' And poor Josip, he is in pain."

It seemed a little silly, but it wasn't silly to Semyon. He was worried. He even decided to go back to the sheds after dinner—even talked Chief Oswiak into flying him down in the copter instead of waiting for the regular trip.

As a consequence, he missed the excitement.

The excitement occurred when the regular copter flight went down. I went along, preferring an evening with the computers to an evening loafing around the wardroom, and Oswiak spotted a running figure in the palmettos as we whirled overhead.

It was not a place where anyone should have been running. We radioed back to Commander Lineback; another copter load of security troops came after us; and in less than ten minutes we landed, encircled, closed in on and recaptured eight Caodai escapees from the stockade, roasting the carcass of a pig over an oven fire.

There were three more pig carcasses in the clearing; they must have worked like demons to get the animals driven off the research area while most of us were at dinner. The security guard hadn't noticed a thing—no doubt because the security guard, relaxed and happy with the sure knowledge that nobody would ever bother a place like Project Mako, was sound asleep under a palm.

Lineback said ruefully: "I guess that's the end of the Pig section of the project. But what bothers me is the radio." It wasn't much of a radio; the sort of thing that prisoners somehow smuggle in, piece by piece; but it could easily have reached out past the horizon to where a Caodai ship might be lurking, barely awash.

Somebody snickered, and Lineback turned on him sharply. "Belay that," he snarled. "Mako might be funny to you, and maybe it's even funny to me. But it isn't funny to COMINCH, because he classified it Most Secret, and he isn't going to like Caodais with radios roaming around it."

"But, Commander," ventured Kedrick, "these guys were just looking for something to eat. They wouldn't have raided the pigs if they'd been after bigger stuff."

"Tell COMINCH," said Lineback shortly. "In fact, that's an order—get it dispatched at once."

Semyon wasn't exactly disappointed at missing the excitement, when I dropped in his section to tell him about it—he had other things on his mind. "Is very bad with Josip," he told me worriedly. "Look!"

All I could see was a slack tail sticking out from under a chair. I said, not too tactfully: "You're lucky. The Pig section is worse off than you—the Caodais ate them up."

I had his full attention. "What?" he demanded, and I had to tell him all about the Caodai escapees again. He kindled like a rocket.

"Curse them!" he raved. "I see it, I see it! They come here to destroy us, Logan! They eat the pigs, they hurt my little dog, heaven only knows what damage they do to the other stock! Call Lineback, Logan! Get him here. No—give me that phone, I will do this myself!"

And he did, he got Lineback there in a matter of minutes. It sounded preposterous, of course, to me and no doubt to Lineback. Still—the Caodais had been in the area, and it was at least something of a coincidence that one of our experimental animals should be in trouble just then. And Josip was in trouble. Seymon managed briefly to coax the dog into his lap, but Josip wasn't happy there. He looked up at us with eyes as big and unhappy as Semyon's. His hindquarters were matted with dried blood; his manner was frightened; he kept making the saddest little whining noises.

I said uncertainly, "Maybe, maybe if we clean him up a little——"

Well, we tried it. Semyon raced down to the head and came back with an armful of paper towels and a dish of water; but Josip wouldn't sit still for us to do it. He jerked convulsively, and moaned and scurried, whining fretfully, under a desk.

By the time Lineback got there, Semyon had worked up a full storm against the Orientals, and he blasted his commanding officer with demands for the instant arrest of every Caodai within reach on grounds of espionage, sabotage and treason.

"Easy, Timiyazev!" rapped Lineback. "What's the story?"

"I am telling it you!" cried Semyon. "My dog has been sabotaged—wounded! Do not believe me, I am only a Russian, a dirty foreigner; do not take my word! But see for yourself!"

He gestured dramatically at the desk.

Lineback looked at us worriedly for a moment. "Oh, hell," he sighed. "The things this Navy makes me do. You say the dog's back there?"

"I say it!"

Lineback reluctantly got down on his hands and knees,

43

had a sudden thought, hesitated and looked at us. "Is he vicious?"

"Josip? Vicious?" Semyon withered Lineback with an unbelieving look.

"All right," said Lineback placatingly, and put his head down to the floor to look under the desk. He suddenly jerked his head up and stared at us; then bent again and reached underneath.

"Do not hurt Josip!" Semyon warned sharply. "He is ill, he has been hurt——"

Lineback's expression was unreadable. He pulled something out from under the desk and held it out to us.

"Mouse!" gasped Semyon. "Poor Josip, he has caught a mouse!"

Lineback shook his head slowly. Then he looked down at the little animal in his cupped hands.

"Not exactly a mouse," he said at last. "It's what we call a puppy. Josip has just given birth to it."

VI

THE NEXT MORNING Commander Lineback sent me down to Miami on orders to pick up equipment. What equipment? Pigs, that's what equipment. Pigs to replace the pigs the Caodai escapees had eaten; and it seemed to me at first that this was Lineback's way of slapping my wrist for the nonsensical business of Josip's puppies, and then it seemed to me that it was his way of rewarding me for the faintly heroic business of the stockade break; and then I stopped worrying about why he was sending me, and took my blessings as they came. For after all, Miami was Miami.

I checked in at a shiny big hotel and presented my orders. The room clerk said, "Glad to have you here, Lieutenant; hope you'll have a good time." He clapped his hands sharply for a bellboy.

I mentioned, "Sergeant, I'm here on official business." He smiled.

The bell captain was an Army corporal. He carried my Val-Pak up to a small but comfortable room and, without thinking about the Navy regulations concerning cash gratuities to military personnel, I gave him a quarter. He didn't give it back. Maybe the Army regulations are different.

My room was thirty stories up, overlooking the ocean and the Gulf Stream. You could almost see the Stream—in fact, I'm not sure but what I did see it, a paler blue in the blue-violet of the inshore waters. You could see quite a lot from my window. You could even see the sooty high-water mark along the white beaches, where the oil from sneak-raid torpedoed tankers had washed ashore.

I changed into my dress greens, left my room key with the tech sergeant at the desk and headed for the headquarters of Commander, South Atlantic Theater.

SP's in white leggings opened the door of my cab and saluted smartly. It was a hotel that made mine look like an outhouse; over its hibiscus-framed front doorway was the stainless-steel legend: COMSOLANT. The word was repeated on the white life preservers that hung from the railings of the walks, on the caps of the elevator operators and the armpatches of the SP's, and was even picked out in pastel tile on the deck around the swimming pool where I was instructed to report.

A petty officer read my orders skeptically, scratched his head and sent one of the SP's to the far end of the pool. A hairy-bodied man in green trunks came back with the SP, toweling himself furiously. "Can't I have even a lunch break, Farragut?" he demanded. "What the devil is it now?"

He read the orders and looked at me irritably. "Mako, Mako," he repeated. "What's Mako?"

I looked quickly at the petty officer. "Classified, sir," I whispered.

He barked, "What the devil isn't?" But he picked up a hush-phone from the petty officer's desk and spoke into it for a moment.

He said: "You're early, Lieutenant. Your commander was distinctly told that the issue wouldn't be ready until Thursday."

I said, "Sorry, sir."

"Oh, not your fault." He gave me back my orders— limp and blurry where he'd dripped on them. "Come back then."

I said: "What shall I do until then, sir?"

He looked at me unbelievingly. "Man," he said, "this is *Miami*. Just be back here Thursday, that's all." And he dove wallowingly into the pool.

So there I was, on my own in Miami. It had been, I counted, seventeen months since I had walked the streets of an American city with time to kill.

On *Spruance*, you didn't take your leave, because where were you going to go? The whole thing about a nuclear-powered submarine cruiser, after all, is that it doesn't need to get back to home base very often. *Spruance* had been cruising for a year when I joined her; she was still cruising when I left.

There had been a couple of times when, for a day or three days, we had touched at Bordeaux or Cork on some strategic errand, and some of us got to stretch our legs ashore. But—have you ever spent a festive evening in a heap of rubble?

Neither has anyone else.

But Miami Beach was festive enough to make up for all. My hotel was bright and shiny, though in the run-down district around Lincoln Road. The wonderful thing about spending a couple of days at the Beach is the pretty girls; for a wise Providence—perhaps a wise COMSOLANT—has put the WAAF hostess-training center right next door in Coral Gables. Biscayne Boulevard is lined with them, seven days a week, all the weeks of the year. Lord knows when the girls find time to study—or perhaps their social life at Biscayne Boulevard is a kind of extension course for the training center, because what else does an airline hostess have to know?

At any rate, they were there—as many as the reminiscing boys on *Spruance* had said, and as pretty. They were the sweetest looking, gayest laughing, homiest seeming things I had seen in seventeen months; and four out of ten of them, seen from a distance, had the same waved brownish hair and carefree walk as Elsie.

Elsie. It was more than two years since we had our last leave together. I stopped under a palm tree and looked, as inconspicuously as I could, at the picture in my wallet. She was almost a stranger. It hadn't been so bad on *Spruance*, where there were few women and there had always been the faint chance of commandoing Zanzibar.

But here in Miami, where everyone but me walked two-by-two, it was bad. I was lonesome.

Her and her cursed volunteering. I had told her and told her, long before her number came up: "When they get you, don't volunteer for *anything*." So naturally she had signed on the courier flight to Nhatrang in Indo-China, where the Caodai Headquarters were, and naturally the courier had wandered off course over Yemen, and naturally the Caodais niked him down. It wasn't Elsie they were interested in; the game they were after was the

47

Air Marshal on whose staff she was a yeoman, a valuable hostage in some future exchange. And they got him. She was lucky she got out in time—and twice as lucky that they'd eventually shipped her to the big internment camp on Zanzibar, along with the marshal.

But me, I was hardly lucky at all.

I had a large glass of fresh orange juice at a sidewalk café and talked with a WAAF at the next table. She was a very attractive blonde; she would have been fun to take out, if she had been Elsie.

I walked two blocks and had a guanabana sherbet at another sidewalk café, and talked with a WAAF sitting next to me at the counter. She was a very attractive brunette, but she wasn't Elsie either.

I considered a third sidewalk café featuring fresh papaya-pineapple drinks. But there is a limit to the amount of liquid I can stand sloshing around in my gut.

Glamorous Miami! I was prepared to sell it short, that hot afternoon.

It wasn't that Miami wasn't very nice. It was too nice for a lonely man. I was battling a sort of perverse, inanimate conspiracy against me on the part of the sun, the sky, the weather. If Elsie had been with me, I would have been happy.

But Elsie was not.

There was only one thing to do. I had been resisting doing it ever since I'd landed at Montauk, en route to Project Mako; I couldn't resist it any more.

I found a phone booth, and the classified book had what I wanted: Hartshorne & Giordano, F.C.C. Licensees, at an address near the Venetian Causeway.

The heading was TELEPATHISTS & ESPERS.

The girl at the desk was an enlisted WAVE. It surprised me, for the last time I had used an esper the whole outfit was aggressively civilian.

She said doubtfully, "Zanzibar? Zanzibar? That's Caodai territory."

"I know it is," I said patiently. "My wife is interned there."

She looked at me as though I were a pacifist or something, but she kept on filling out the forms. I gave her all the information she asked for, and she said:

"You're lucky. They say that all ESP communication will be pre-empted for military use the first of the month. Now, would you like this guaranteed or not?"

"Non-guaranteed," I said. The difference in the rate was considerable, and besides I'd had half a dozen previous rapports with Elsie. There wasn't any doubt in my mind that I'd get through, that is if she was still——

Never mind *that*, I told myself quickly, and listened to the WAVE. She was mumbling figures from a rate book and making marks on a pad.

"Eleven dollars and ninety-five cents, including tax," she said at last. "That's for three minutes." She spoke into an intercom, and nodded to me. "Mr. Giordano will see you now," she said.

Giordano was a beady-eyed little old man with curly white hair. "Six previous rapports," he said approvingly, studying my chart. "Well, ten cc ought to be enough for you. Will you roll up your sleeves, please?"

I looked away as the needle bit into my arm. It tingled; the hormone solution you take before an esper rapport seems to be distilled from wasp venom. "Thank you," he said, and I rolled down my sleeve as he sat down at his desk. He wasn't much like the last esper I'd gone to, back in Providence when Elsie was first interned; that particular one had worn a white tunic with a side-buttoned collar like a surgeon's, and he had been a phony from the word go. Oh, he put me in touch with Elsie all right, but there had been a gauzy shapelessness about the contact that had left me more unsatisfied when I left than when I came in.

This one had a fine businesslike air about him; he wore an ordinary Navy undress uniform with a Chief Warrant's pin in his collar. That's a more important factor in esping than most people realize. The Providence hookup had

49

been the one real failure I had had with Elsie.

"May I have the node, Lieutenant?" he asked.

The "node" was the photograph of Elsie from my wallet. He studied it approvingly. Why is it that the photograph one carries of a girl is always in a bathing suit? Is it that the more you can see of a subject, the more vividly the silver agglutinates bring her back? Or just that one carries a camera to the beach?

"Very nice," he said. "Now, how about your nodal experience?"

"Well," I said hesitantly, "how about this one? Just before the picture was taken, we had lunch on a terrace overlooking the beach. There was a band, and we danced."

"And you remember the tune the band was playing?" I nodded. "Good. One other thing, Lieutenant. Do you know what time it is in Zanzibar now?"

I snapped my fingers. "Oh, damn. She'll be asleep?"

He glanced at a chart and nodded. "It's around two in the morning there. Of course, you can get rapport even if she's asleep, you know, but she may not remember it in the morning or she may think it's a dream."

I said: "We'll try it." I could always try again the next day, I told myself; the money didn't matter.

"Lean back," he said gently, and the lights went out, all but a tiny, indirect one that softened the shadows but left nothing for the mind to fix on.

I felt the esper come into my mind. I know that some people find that an ordeal, like the dentist's pick prying into the bicuspid; for me it has always been a warming, protecting sort of coming-together. Perhaps it is because I've never esped anyone but Elsie, and it hasn't been a matter of exchanging data but of moods. Those who try to use espers for business calls, trying to pinpoint details in that cloudly contact, must find the whole process exasperating.

I heard, in the back of my mind, the slow whispers of the music, and I saw the beach-umbrellaed terrace where Elsie and I had danced. The esper was finding the range.

Elsie? I formed the name in my mind.

50

She was asleep, all right. But her voice from faraway, foggy but real: Darling.

In succession I formed the thoughts: I'm well. I'm lonesome. I love you.

And her answers: I'm well, but tired. I love you too. I want to see you.

Three minutes went very fast.

What had I accomplished?

Nothing, perhaps. Nothing that could have been put on a progress report. I didn't know why Elsie was tired; I didn't know what she had had for dinner, or what the weather was in Zanzibar. I didn't even have a phrase or a gesture or a look to treasure; nothing that had been that clear. Esping is a form of communication, certainly, but of emotions rather than concepts. One speaks with sighs instead of syllables, and I don't know any answer to give to those who say you can get the same effect staring into the bubbles in your beer. For a moment I had been with Elsie in my mind. I couldn't touch her; I couldn't hear her, taste her, smell her or see her; but she was there. Was that worth slightly more than six cents a second, tax included?

It was worth anything in the world, for a man in my circumstances.

I paid the girl at the desk dreamily, and drifted out. I was halfway across the street before I heard her calling after me.

"Hey, Lieutenant! You forgot your hat." I took it from her, blinking. She said: "I hope things work out for you and your wife."

I thanked her and caught a bus back along the palm-lined boulevards.

All the depression was gone. All right, I hadn't touched Elsie—but I had been with her. How many times, after all, in our short married life together had I waked in the night and known, only known, that she was asleep beside me? I didn't have to wake her, or talk to her, or turn on the light and look at her; I knew she was there.

I got off the bus at Lincoln Road, still dreaming. It was

dark, or nearly so, before I came to and realized that I had walked far past my hotel and I was hungry.

I looked around for a place to eat, but I was in an area of solid brass. COMSOLANT was only a block away, and the two nearest restaurants bore the discreet legend: *Flag Officers Only.*

I turned around and walked back toward my own area.

I wondered why it was so dark, and then realized that Miami Beach, like Project Mako, was blacked out. But it seemed blacker than a blackout could account for, and not in any understandable way. The lights were there, hidden behind their canvas shields from the possible enemy eyes at sea; not very many of them and not very bright, but they were there. The narrow slits in the shields over the street lamps cast enough light on the pavement for me to see where my feet were going. The cars that moved along the boulevards had their marker lights, dim and downward cast, but clear. And yet I was finding it hard to get my bearings.

Something was sawing at my mind.

It was the hormone shots, I thought, with a feeling of relief; I was still a little sensitive, perhaps, from the esping. What I needed was a good meal and to sit down for a while; it would make me as good as new.

But where was a restaurant?

Someone slid a burning pine splinter into the base of my neck. It hurt very much.

I must have yelled, because figures came running toward me. I couldn't see them very clearly, and not only because of the darkness; and I couldn't quite hear what they said, because something was whining and droning in my ears, or in my mind.

There was another stab at the base of my head, and one in my shoulders, like white-hot knives. I felt myself falling; something smacked across my face, and I knew it was the pavement. But that pain was numbed and nothing, compared to the fire stabbing into my neck and shoulders.

Someone was tugging at my arm and roaring. I heard a

police whistle and wondered why; and then I didn't wonder anything for a while. The world was black and silent; even the pain was gone.

VII

"——still alive, for God's sake! Suppose we ought to let him sleep it off?"

I pushed someone's slapping hands away from me and opened one eye.

Ringed around me were half a dozen faces, looking down—a couple of nurses, a doctor or two, and a j.g. with a thin black mustache and an OOD band on his arm.

"Well," said the Officer of the Deck, "welcome back."

I tasted something awful in my mouth. "Wha— what happened?"

The faces were grave. "You got burned."

Apparently being burned was no laughing matter. I groggily made sense of what they were telling me.

Like the Air Force captain at the Boca Raton field, like the other mysterious victims I had heard whispers about —I had been burned. And it was true enough; they showed me a bright mirror above, and I could see the burns. My shoulders, the base of my neck, a thin line down my back; they were all brilliant scarlet, like a bad sunburn; and they hurt.

Something clicked in my fuzzy brain. "Oh," I said, "the Glotch."

But they had never heard of "the Glotch." Evidently the Boca Raton name for it was purely local, but the thing was the same, all right. They called it "getting burned"; the OOD, whose name was Barney Savidge, had heard it called "the Caodai horrors." But it was all the same thing, and all bad. "You're a lucky kid," said Lieutenant Savidge. "We picked you up and it looked like you were as dead as the rest of them. After all, only one out of a thous——"

"Savidge!" one of the medics said sharply.

The OOD looked guilty. "Sorry, sir," he said. "Anyway, Miller, you're lucky."

They wouldn't tell me much; apparently the Glotch was as hush-hush in Miami as it was in Boca Raton.

But it appeared I would live. They brought me coffee after they finished dressing my burns. I was in COM-CARIB's naval hospital, and, although I had visions of being a celebrity for a day, the OOD cut me down to size. "It comes and goes," he said, looking apprehensively at the ship's surgeon out of earshot across the room. "It comes and goes, some days a whole bunch of casualties, some days none. Last night was one of the bad ones."

"You mean I wasn't the only one?"

"Hah! There were seven, Miller—last I heard." He stared at me thoughtfully. "The only difference between you and the other six is, you're alive."

It was a cheerful thought. "Well," I said, "thanks for everything and I guess I'll be getting along——"

"I guess you won't," he said sharply. "Maybe in the morning. They want to look you over—after all, you're supposed to be dead, you know. They want to find out how come you're not."

It wasn't so bad. They kept taking my temperature for a while, and feeling my pulse, and talking to each other in what doctors use for English. But Savidge, who didn't appear to be too overworked as OOD, dropped in every few minutes and we got fairly well acquainted; and along about three in the morning they decided I could go to sleep.

So I did; but I wouldn't say I slept well.

The hairy-bodied officer at COMSOLANT was in uniform this time, and he turned out to be a captain. "Miller," he said crisply, "I told you your stuff wasn't ready yet. Are you trying to rush me?"

"No sir, but——"

"But go away, Miller" he said persuasively. "Remember the famous motto of the Navy: 'Don't call me, I'll call you.' You're dismissed." And that was that.

I wandered down to COMCARIB and rousted Barney Savidge out of bed. He was bleary-eyed on three hours sleep after a night as Officer of the Deck, but he began to wake up with the third cup of wardroom coffee. "I'll tell you what we do," he began to plan. "We'll pick up a couple of WAAFs from the training center and run over to Tropical Park for the afternoon and——"

"I'm married, Barney."

He stared at me. "What?"

"I don't want to pick up a couple of WAAFs," I explained.

He scratched his head. "Well," he said after a moment, "we'll go over to Tropical Park by ourselves and——"

I said: "Barney, could we look around the base here? I've been out on a dairy—that is," I corrected myself hurriedly, remembering those bright red Most Secret stamps on my travel orders, "I've been out of touch with the Navy. Let's take a look at the ships."

All he said was: "It takes all kinds."

COMCARIB is only a satellite of COMSOLANT, but the Caribbean fleet is big enough for anybody. There were forty men-of-war surfaced in Biscayne Bay, destroyers and carriers and a couple of *Nimitz*-class cruisers that brought a curious sensation to my throat. "Busy out there," I said, staring hungrily at the fighting ships nursing from the tankers.

"It's getting busier all the time, Logan," Barney said soberly. "See that bucket beyond the breakwater?" He was pointing at an ancient monitor, a harbor defense craft with plenty of punch but no range to speak of. Work barges were lashed to its sides and welders were slicing into a twisted, scarred mass of metal on its forward deck.

"Looks like it tangled with a can opener," I said.

"A Caodai can opener. That's *Hadley*, and it was down off the Keys when a Caodai sneak raid took a potshot at it. It got back; there were two last month that didn't."

I said uneasily, "Barney, have things been hotting up while I was at sea? All this business of getting burned and sneak raids right off our coast—it sounds bad."

Barney shrugged morosely. "Who knows? There isn't any war on."

"No, really," I insisted. "What's the score?"

"Who knows?" he repeated. "You can see for yourself, things are happening. Up until last year, COMCARIB had never lost a capital ship in coastal waters. Since then —well, never mind how many. But we've lost some. Are things getting worse all over, or is it just local? I don't know. We send out a squad of scout torpedoes three times a day, and I guess we average twenty contacts a week. By the time the big boys get to where the torpedoes have made a contact, there's nothing there, usually. Sometimes not even the scout. But you look in the papers and you find nothing about it, of course. Once in a while, maybe, there's a story about 'Unidentified vessel sighted off Miami Beach'—that's when you can see them from the top floor windows of the hotels. But that's all."

He flicked his cigarette into the water and grinned at me. "Now do we go to Tropical Park?" he demanded.

So we went, and I succeeded in losing forty-five dollars. It wasn't hard. I just bet my hunches. By the fourth race the T/5 at the five-dollar window got to know me and shook his head sadly when I bought my tickets; but I didn't mind much, because what I was thinking of was not horses and pari-mutuel betting but war and Elsie.

I sat out the sixth race in a canteen under the grandstand and read a newspaper. I could hear the crowd screaming and stamping overhead, but the newspaper thundered louder than they, if only you read between the lines. *Eight-Year-Olds Face Student Draft.* How long had we been putting school kids in uniform? Had it started while I was on *Spruance?* The age limits had been going lower and lower, that much I knew—but eight-year-olds? I tried to remember exactly when it was that they had called up the Boy Scouts and made them an integral, draft-manned part of the defense apparatus, with civil-defense functions and a co-ordinated pre-induction training program. *Caodais Protest Ankara Looting, Threaten Reprisals Against Hostages.* I read that one thoroughly. There had been trouble at the Caodai legislation in Turkey, and the Caodais appeared to think it was deliberately fomented. That much was simple enough, but the bit about hostages gave me a bad time.

Because I couldn't help remembering that one of the

57

hostages was no mere statistic, but the girl I had married.

The nature of the trouble in Ankara was far from clear; sometimes it seemed to me that there had been an arson attempt, sometimes a mere hit and run burglary. It was sloppy reporting, and I read the item over a dozen times before I concluded that it didn't matter; if the Caodais were looking for a pretext to take their temper out on their hostages, anything at all would serve.

I found Barney in the crowd, right where I'd left him, and told him my burns were bothering me. It was true enough, at that; my whole neck was stiffening up; but what was bothering me most of all was life itself. I arranged to meet him again and caught the bus back to my hotel, so lost in my own ugly thoughts that I didn't pay any attention to the desk clerk's expression.

But what he handed me along with my room key jolted me out of my reverie. It was a mailgram from Project Mako: LEAVE CANCELED. RETURN PROJECT IMMEDIATELY. LINEBACK

VIII

KEDRICK FUSSED over me like a furious kitten. "Curse it, Miller, don't you know the first thing about military security? You've got your head crammed full of the top classified information in the country—and you have to blather it all over the world with an *esper*."

I swallowed and said nothing at all. In truth, the attack on the beach had made me nearly forget about going to the esper.

"Answer me!" shouted Kendrick.

. I hadn't heard the question. But that didn't make much difference. "I'm sorry, sir," I said.

"Sorry!" Kedrick seemed to inflate with pent-up irritation. "Sorry! If you're sorry now, what will you be when a court-martial gets hold of you?"

I stammered, "But I—I didn't *say* anything, sir. I just sort of, well, wanted to know how my wife was. You don't *talk* when you esp, you just——"

"Knock it off," ordered Kedrick explosively. "You can tell all that to Commander Lineback. I can assure you, though, that he takes a dim view of you right at the moment."

"Yes, sir."

I appeared to be dismissed, so I started a rather stiff-armed salute. It attracted Kedrick's attention.

"What the devil's the matter with your neck?" he demanded.

I touched the bandages. "What you call the Glotch, sir," I said, and told him my adventure. It took a lot of the passion out of him. He was staring pensively at nothing when I finished.

"Is that all, sir?" I said politely, after a moment.

"What?" He roused himself and said heavily, "Oh, I guess so, Miller. This is a crazy business."

"Yes, sir," I agreed.

He seemed very tired all of a sudden, but he scratched

his head and said: "You're dismissed. Have a drink or two and——"

"I don't drink, sir," I said.

"Well, pop a couple and get a night's sleep." He shook his head wearily. "Trouble!" he meditated. "The Glotch and the stockade getting set to explode and wet-nursed jaygees spilling their guts with espers——" He was talking to himself, not me. I saluted and hit the sack. I hadn't fully understood the reference to the stockade, but I didn't let worry keep me awake; I dreamed very happily of Elsie until the mess attendant tapped on my door at 0700.

Lineback was broody after that. He was worried about the esper and the possibility of Caodai transmission from the little radio the escapees had, I suppose; but he was also rather strained in his relations with Semyon and me. You can't blame him. He came to his position as head of Project Mako by the animal-husbandry route, and he must have been astonished to find how little we animal experts knew about animals.

I don't say it was punishment, but the next time the officers' extra-duty roster was posted, Semyon and I were prominent on it: *To assist Project Veterinary Officer,* it said after our names. Of course, "extra duty" is defined as that which you do after all your regular duties are well taken care of; that meant I spent the time from 0800 to 1600 running my RAGNAROK while Semyon worked with his dogs—including Josip, now renamed Josie, and her pups. Then, promptly after dinner, we reported to the veterinarian's office for a pleasant evening's relaxation.

And the veterinarian handed us a small box of thermometers with which to perform our duties.

It was, I told Semyon later on in the milk shed, a lousy way to fight a cold war.

"Cattle!" complained Semyon. "If it could be only at least a dog, which I know well, you understand, and like. . . . But cattle! Shoo!" And we poked under the tails of resentful cows, though the cows were no more resentful than I. For all his grousing, Semyon was not unhappy with

60

the job; so I turned the temperature-taking segment of it over to him, and myself took the daily check-chart to record his findings. It was, I reminded myself, important work; Lineback had said so himself, too important to entrust to an enlisted man. But it didn't *seem* like important work. I wondered what Elsie would think if she saw me squatting soberly on a bale of hay, while the world crept closer to the point of ignition. Elsie. I stared out at the brilliant white moon that, ten hours before, had been shining on Elsie, and I missed my wife very much. . . .

"Logan! I have been talking to you!"

"Sorry, Semyon." He was looking worried; he waved the thermometer at me.

"Three of them, Logan! I examine three cattle, and they are hot. Epidemic, no? So I examine two more, and they are hot, too!"

I looked at the chart—it was true, I had written it myself but had hardly noticed what I was writing. Semyon had taken the temperature of five cows, and they all hovered a bit over 100 degrees.

I said: "It's not much of a fever, Semyon——"

"Call Lineback."

"But, listen, Semyon——"

"Call Lineback."

I called Lineback, getting him out of a pleasant bridge game at the club. "Sir, we've got some sick cattle here. They all have fevers, every one of them." And Semyon was chattering over my shoulder about the Orientals and secret germ weapons; Lineback sounded mad. But he promised to come right over.

And he did, with the veterinary officer at his side. And that, children, is when I first learned that the normal temperature of a healthy cow is not 98-plus degrees, but 101.

It was still a brilliant full moon as Semyon and I limped back to quarters, nursing our wounds; but I wasn't enjoying it. Commander Lineback had been pretty rough.

"Ah, well," said Semyon philosophically, "at least we do not have that detail any more."

61

I told him to shut up. But gradually I was soothed. The clouds, white and fleecy in the moonlight; a mutter of thunder from over the Gulf Stream; a gentle, warm wind —it was pleasant. I sighed. Semyon looked at me. "You are thinking of your wife?"

"What?" I started to shake my head; but then I realized it was true—not with the top of my mind, no, but deep inside. "It's been a long time," I said.

"Ah, perhaps. Two years, is it? That is not so terribly long."

"It's long enough for me," I said shortly. "I wouldn't mind so much, if I were doing anything to shorten it."

We walked along for a moment; but the night was no longer so pleasant. "The trouble is not hearing anything," I told him after a moment. "No letters. No more esping— Lineback'd put me in irons if I tried it again."

"Terrible," he agreed.

"And no chance in the world of ever getting anywhere near her. Semyon," I said sincerely, "that's the worst thing. At least when I was on the cruiser there was always the chance——"

"Lieutenant Miller?"

It was a runner from the commander's staff, peering at us through the moonlight.

"Yes?"

Commander's compliments," he said breathlessly, "and will you report to him at the milk shed—on the double?"

"Oh-oh," said Semyon. We looked at each other. What was Lineback doing back at the milk shed?

There was only one way to find out. We went back to the shed—perhaps not exactly on the double, but near enough to it so that we were both breathing hard.

Lineback, the vet and a couple of other officers were a circle of bobbing torches in the darkness—not in the shed, but behind it, gathered around—a sick cow? Something on the ground, anyway. I couldn't quite see.

Kedrick flashed his light in my face. "Miller," he said, "take a look." For once he wasn't fussy, he wasn't an old maid. His torch shone on what was on the ground.

It wasn't a cow, it was a man. Or at any rate—it had been.

"Oswiak," I said. But it wasn't easy to recognize him; the chin, the throat, one whole side of the jawline, all were horribly burned and tortured. He was dead, and he hadn't died easily. "The Glotch."

"The Glotch," said Kedrick. "You were here before. Any ideas about this?"

The only idea I had was to get away from that face—it reminded me of how close I had come, back in Miami. I said so.

Lineback sighed heavily, and I could hear him scratching his long jaw in the darkness. "So they've spotted Mako," he said. "Somebody's going to catch bloody blue hell for this. Well, let's get him to the sick bay, you medics."

I didn't stop in the wardroom; I went right to bed, but not immediately to sleep. Oswiak's face was too clear before me.

It isn't that I'm particularly queasy. I've seen dead men more times than one. I've been close enough to dying myself, not only in Miami, not only in the action after the stockade break, but on *Spruance*.

But Oswiak had been *burned;* and there is something especially repellent about a man who has died of burns, yards from anywhere, in the middle of a healthy, unsinged stand of crab grass. It wasn't natural; it wasn't decent.

I swore at Semyon when he tried to wake me for breakfast, and slept right through until he came back to the room just before lunch. By then, of course, he knew as much as I did—he and all the rest of Project Mako, all the more because Commander Lineback had put out an order-of-the-day placing the whole subject under top secret classification. Naturally, that insured that every officer and rating on the project had to find out just what it was that was secret; but it made it possible for me to duck discussing it with Semyon, who had a somber interest in such matters.

It wasn't much of a working day for me. I went down

63

to my workroom after lunch, but I wasn't there half an hour when the usual rating appeared with the usual compliments-and-get-the-devil-down-here from Lineback.

This time, for a novelty, he seemed almost sympathetic. "I've been talking to COMBARI," he said abruptly. "You're in trouble, Miller."

"Yes, sir," I said.

"That's nothing new, eh? Well, you're right; it's nothing new. I've had you on this carpet before about using Giordano to get in touch with your wife, and that's what you're in trouble about today. However, I'm sorry to say that you're in a little more trouble now."

I said, "Yes, sir."

"You damned young fool!" he exploded. "How does it feel to have killed a man, Miller?"

That startled me. "*Killed*—"

"Or the next thing to it. You saw him last night, Chief Oswiak, with his throat burned out."

I screamed, "That's not *fair*, Commander! I—"

"*Shut up, Miller.*" He got control of himself with a visible effort. "You didn't do anything on purpose, no. In fact, you don't do much on purpose ever, do you? You blunder into things. Like you blundered into this one—and killed off a CPO. Ah," he finished moodily, "the hell with it. I just called you in here to tell you what COMCARIB said. *If* those burns are a Caodai secret weapon—there's small doubt of it, Miller—there's evidence that they are linked with ESP transmission. From Project Mako, I guarantee, there has been absolutely no ESP transmission. Except once—not from here, but from Miami, when I didn't have my eyes on you for a moment; and that transmission was from you."

There was more, but it didn't matter. He reamed me out and through and up and down; but it didn't hurt very much because I was numb. I did not enjoy the thought that, however stupidly and unwittingly, I had helped the Cow-dyes kill an American.

"—there won't be any court-martial," he was finishing, and I focused on him again. "But you deserve it,

64

Miller, and I want you to know that from here until you leave this base, I'm watching you."

That seemed to be that. I said, "Yes, sir," automatically, and saluted, and turned to leave.

But he wasn't quite finished. "One more thing," he said, his expression unreadable. "I picked up a piece of information that you might be interested in. You were on *Spruance* before you came here, weren't you?"

"Yes, sir."

"Then you might be interested to know that this burning gizmo the Caodais have has just been tested out on a submerged vessel. The Caodais are probably pretty happy, because according to a burst transmission COMCARIB intercepted it works. The whole engineering section of the sub died at once, and the sub hasn't been heard from since." He looked at me levelly. "It was *Spruance*, Miller."

I had thought I was numb, but I wasn't quite numb enough. I was out in the anteroom, ignoring Giordano sitting there reproachfully, waiting for his own turn under the lash, before it occurred to me to wonder if I had saluted.

Spruance was sunk.

And I was tending cows and pushing buttons in a featherbed project ashore.

IX

THERE HAD BEEN big doings down in the bay for a couple of weeks, but we had been warned to keep our noses out of it. Something had been floated in on a moonlit night, guarded by a patrol boat, convoyed by two little Diesel tugs; and a huge tarpaulin tent had been erected over it, and Navy mechanics had been hammering at it day and night. They weren't our own mechanics; they were flown in in shifts, and flown out again, even for mess.

Semyon and I strolled down one evening after work, but a husky seaman with a rifle leaned out of a cluster of palmettos and chased us. We didn't argue; I heard the snick of the bolt on his rifle, and we turned around and went home. "Very silly procedure," Semyon said angrily. "They might have shot us!"

"I think they would have," I said. The seaman had looked very businesslike.

"Barbarous!" raged Semyon. "In Irkutsk such a thing would not be. Ah, Logan, you Americans have not yet learned the proper conduct of a war. In Krasnoye Army when I was a cadet at the Suvorov Academy——"

"I've heard," I said. "And what is Krasnoye Army doing today?"

"Oh, granted." Semyon agreed cheerfully. "You beat the ears from us; we lost. True. But, Logan, we lost so *well!*"

"Let's go into town," I said disgustedly.

We took a copter to Boca Raton and wandered around at loose ends. "Let's go to the Passion Pit," Semyon suggested eagerly.

"Why not?" It wasn't my idea of a big evening, but I admittedly didn't have any better ideas to suggest. Besides, I had been a long time away from Elsie, but not quite long enough to be looking for another girl; and in spite of its name the Passion Pit was about the most innocuous spot in town. They didn't even have a license; if

66

you wanted to get high in the Passion Pit, you brought your own.

We paid our admission fee, stood still while the attendant stamped our foreheads with fluorescent ink—so that we could walk in and out, if we wished, without being able to crash the place unpaid; the UV spotlight at the door showed who had paid his admission, and who was merely hopeful of getting in for free—and sat down to watch the floor show. "We should have brought a couple of shots," Semyon grumbled. "It is not fun, just sitting here. If I wish to see cows cavort, there are plenty at Proj——"

"Shut up." It wasn't only that I wanted to keep him from mentioning Project Mako by name, though we'd had pretty stiff orders about that; but the chorus girls were near enough to hear, and one of them was glaring at us.

"All right. But we should have brought a couple of shots."

I shrugged. Semyon didn't pop and I didn't drink—we'd had arguments about it—but there wasn't any sense discussing it with him. Anyway, the Pit was filling up and if we went out for a shot we wouldn't be likely to get our seats back.

The Passion Pit wasn't anything like a pit, really; it was on the beach, looking out over the ocean; it was only the size of it and the way the crowd acted on a busy night that gave it its name. I suppose seventy-five people could have fitted into it comfortably. On a dull Monday it usually held a hundred. The tables were more than merely close, they almost touched each other, and where you fitted in your chairs was your own problem.

Semyon nudged me and pointed. He had a thunderhead scowl, and I saw why. Over against the wall, decorously eating in the midst of the uproar, ignoring the band blaring in their ears and the chorus line kicking past their noses, sat Commander Lineback and a dowdy middle-aged WAVE j.g. "Even here he follows us!" hissed Semyon.

"Don't mind him," I said. "Who's the woman?"

"Semyon pursed his lips. "You have never met the officer, his wife? A very charming lady—almost as charming as this who comes now!" He swiveled his chair around, eyes gleaming, completely forgetting about the commander and his lady. The feature stripper of the evening was making her appearance. She was new, but I had heard of her. She was actually a commissioned officer, which meant talent a good cut above the usual level of the Passion Pit, most of whose entertainers were lucky to hope to make CPO. I flagged a waiter and ordered beer—the best you could do in the Pit—and sat back to enjoy myself.

But it was not to be. The three-piece "orchestra" had just begun the slow, deep-beat number that the stripper worked to when fireworks began going off outside. Sirens blared and search beams lashed the sky, and shots and signal rockets and more commotion than New Year's Eve in a madhouse. Semyon said something startled and violent in Russian, and we craned our necks to see out the window.

Something was going on down at the beach, but we could not see precisely what. "Let us go look," Semyon proposed gleefully. "Perhaps they have caught a patchifist."

"Pacifist. But I just ordered a beer, and the show——"

"Logan, there is no show," he said severely. He was right; the stripper was standing at the window, staring out; the musicians were right behind her. It was more exciting outside the Passion Pit than in, at that. Half the population of the town seemed to be beating the waterfront. "Let us look!"

He wasn't the only one with that idea. We joined the throng beating its way down to the scene of the excitement. It was a fine, warm night, smelling of hibiscus and decaying palms, not fitting for so much turmoil. "Patchifist, patchifist!" Semyon was bawling; and whether he was the first to have the idea or not I cannot say, but in a moment it seemed that the whole town was screaming, "Lynch the dirty pacifists! String 'em up!"

68

It was a frightening exhibition of mob violence, erupting out of nothing, driving remorselessly to a bloody goal. I had seen a lynching like this one once before, back in New York, when ten square miles of countryside converged to dip one man by his heels into his own cistern. It turned out later that the original trouble has been over land and the man was no more a pacifist than you or I, only a queer, moody sort of recluse from the city; but that must have been little enough consolation to him when the rope broke. Not that I doubted that pacifists, and dangerous ones, really existed; but there had been no pacifist there in Barton.

And there was none here. The crowd surged to the water's edge and stopped.

In a writhing heap on a baggage cart, covered with a blanket, was a casualty of the cold war. An Army medical colonel was beside him, methodically injecting a series of drugs into an arm that was held by two sick-faced men. The injured man was unconscious and he wasn't screaming; but he was in pain.

Someone in authority was questioning the colonel. The medic shrugged without looking up. "I don't know," he said. "Obstetrics is my specialty, but I think he'll be all right. No, I don't know what did it. He was on harbor patrol, es——"

He looked up, and a curtain descended over his face. "You'll have to ask somebody else," he said shortly. He waved at the fireworks out over the water. "They've found something, that's all I know."

They had found it, all right; there were more light Navy vessels, mostly high-speed hydrofoils, skimming over the water than I had seen since the Fleet exercises. The show went on for half an hour before we found out just what it was that they had discovered.

They brought him in on an airscrew hydrofoil, zooming up to the landing, stopping short as the screws were reversed, sinking down on the foils to its hull lines just at the dock—a real hot-pilot operation. Semyon and I had pulled rank to get onto the landing itself, and we were

69

right there when the hydrofoil's crew handed him up.

He was a little fellow, not more than five-two or there-abouts, brown skinned and olive eyed. He was dead. He wore breathing gear and frog flippers on his feet, and around his waist was a whole assembly line of weapons and equipment.

It was the first Caodai I had ever seen dead in that way. But it was not the first body I had seen, pitted and scarred, looking like the bottom man on a pile of football players, run over by a team with white-hot cleats on their shoes; and when I saw the wounds on the Caodai frogman's back and neck I knew what had been wrong with the injured man at the waterfront. He had lived, but the Caodai had not, any more than the CPO at Mako had.

Secret weapon? But if the Caodais owned it, how had it destroyed one of their own men?

We never did go back to the Passion Pit; it didn't seem like a good idea any more. We went home and to bed; and the next morning Commander Lineback had me in his office again.

"I saw you on the raft last night, Miller," he began heavily, and I braced myself for what might be coming. He passed a hand over his face. "I don't know, boy," he said querulously. "I don't think there's anything wrong with you. Heaven knows I don't think you're a Cow-dye spy or anything like that, but why is it that whenever anything goes wrong you're right on the scene?"

I said, "Sir, Lieutenant Timiyazev and I were in the Pa—"

"I know. I saw you." He shook his head and said kindly: "Look, Miller, will you just try to stay out of trouble for a while? I've got work for you."

"Yes, sir, but——"

"Forget it." He pressed a button and a rating came in with what looked like an old-fashioned pilot's helmet, one of those close fitting things with earflaps that the old open-cockpit boys wore as a badge of office, except that this

70

one seemed to be woven of shiny aluminum. "Try it on," the commander invited. "It's for you."

I put it on without comment; it squeezed my ears a little, but it wasn't too bad. Lineback half smiled. "It doesn't do much for your looks," he observed. "We'll see if it helps keep you alive."

"Alive, sir?"

He said, "You saw that Cow-dye last night."

I swallowed, and looked at the helmet again, turning it over in my hands. "Put it back on," he ordered sharply. "Until further notice you'll wear it twenty-four hours a day, every day, all day. That's an order."

I put it back on. "Why me, sir?" I asked.

The commander lit a cigarette and waved out the match. "I think I told you that the weapon is linked with ESP. You've been esp-sensitized. *Every victim so far has been sensitized.* COMCARIB thinks that means that if you haven't been sensitized, you aren't susceptible to the Cow-dye weapon—whatever it is. You'll find a lot of them on the project, starting today; you're the first."

"Thanks," I said. He only glanced at me, and I added, "Sir."

He said mildly, "You did see that Cow-dye, didn't you?"

I had, and if the aluminum hat would keep me from looking like him, I would wear the aluminum hat. But something was bothering me. I said, "If it's a Caodai weapon, sir, how come it hit him?"

Lineback shrugged. "Maybe COMCARIB knows, but if so they haven't seen fit to inform me. All I know is that a seaman on harbor patrol—an esper, as it happened—reported detecting Cow-dye ESP off the shore. He alerted the harbor patrol, and before they got on the scent he was slugged with—with whatever it is. Radiation, I suppose. They say he'll live, by the way. I imagine the weapon backfired. They couldn't find any trace of a gun or anything like that. Maybe it was portable, and the Cow-dye dropped it when he was hurt. Anyway, they're dragging

71

—in five hundred feet of water, so don't hold your breath till they find anything." Lineback shook himself. "Enough of this conversation," he said. "I said I've got work for you."

I assumed a posture of attention. "Yes, sir!" I said, trying to look as military as possible.

A new batch of bright animal sayings to process through the computer, I thought, or perhaps some pleasant little additional duty with the thermometers. If I had to take that sort of thing to stay in the Navy I would take it; but at least I would try to be shipshape about it. I leaned forward and picked up the sealed orders Lineback flipped across the desk to me.

But it wasn't like that at all. I opened them and stared in utter disbelief.

I was ordered to assume command of a sea-going fighting ship!

For a moment I felt as though I were in the real honest-to-John-Paul-Jones Navy again.

But only for a moment, because when Semyon and I raced down to examine my new command we discovered that there had been a few little modifications. MHV *Weems* was a deep-sea heavy monitor, 6,000 tons displacement, nuclear-powered, armed with 20 homing-torpedo tubes and damned little else. *Weems* was an elderly lady by the time COMCARIB turned her over to me, but monitors of her class had served well and damagingly to the enemy in a great many actions, and she still could have been a command worth having—especially for a j.g.

However, COMCARIB's engineers had performed a sort of crude hysterectomy on the old girl. She didn't look much different, under the tarpaulin tent, but her torpedo racks were empty, the tubes were plugged with steel disks, and far-reaching changes had been made in her propulsion system. For one thing, four inches of sheathing had been stripped from her reactor. It made a nice economy in weight—*Weems*, from a lumbering snail of a vessel, could now in theory lope along as lightly as a corvette—but it had the one drawback that everybody inside her

72

hull was subject to a gentle wash of radiation all the time the reactor was going.

Semyon looked at me with the roundest of eyes. "Logan," he gasped, "are they making a kamikaze of you?"

"Of us," I said, grimly enjoying myself. "You're part of my crew."

"I am *not*," he yelped. "In Krasnoye Army is never——"

"It's all right," I assured him. "Relax! In the first place, this old wagon isn't going anywhere; in the second place, if it did, and you and I went with it, we would live up forward in a sealed whaleboat. When the reactor was on, we'd be behind a six-inch bulkhead; the only communication we would have with the main compartments would be over the intercoms."

He meditated. "*Otchi khorashaw*," he announced. "Is all right." He patted the heavy tube-loading gear, still in place because it was too clumsy to take out. "Is not bad, this *Weems*," he said thoughtfully. "And you are commander. I congratulate you, Logan."

We toured the ship like midshipmen on their first training cruise. Semyon was delighted with the happy combination of sea and shore duty; we would spend our working days on *Weems*, sleep in our quarters ashore, have our evenings free for the Passion Pit. He had it all figured out . . .

Almost all.

The whaleboat which would nominally be our quarters was comfortable enough, though not large; it was similar in design to the scout torpedoes I had piloted when I was attached to *Spruance*, but not as fast and not armed. Its whole function was to get a part of the crew away in case the monitor was crippled or breached. There were quarters for three: A "captain's cabin"—mine—the principal distinction of which was a curtain to draw across the bunk; and two uncurtained bunks fitted around the main drive shaft. It would be a little cramped on an extended cruise; but livable.

Something was troubling Semyon. We tramped aft

73

from the sealing hatch to the whaleboat, and he cast puzzled looks at the main control board, the fire control panel, the complicated fighting gear of a deep-sea monitor. COMCARIB's engineers had been busiest here. Most of the panel had been made fully automatic, run off a modified baby computer; what little could not be automatized had been redesigned. Push buttons had been replaced with big, soft-handled throw switches. Infinite-range microverniers had been ripped out, and simple on-off two-position toggles put in their place. There could be little grace or flexibility in operating *Weems* with the new controls; power ahead would be "Full" or "Dead Stop"; rudder would be hard right or amidships.

But it would go.

Semyon started to ask me a question a couple of times, but frowned and stopped himself each time. It was only when we came to where the crew quarters should have been that he exploded. "Logan," he said accusingly, "there is something here which is not right! Where are the bunks, Logan? What is this canvas on the floor, Logan? Why is there no galley on this *Weems*, Logan?"

I nodded. "You can figure it out," I told him. "You realize this whole area of the ship would be awash with radiation in action."

"Of course! That is why I ask, Logan!"

I said: "Everything simple, even a child could operate it. Maybe less than a child, even, Semyon." He was staring at me. I said swiftly: "Now perhaps you know what Project Mako was all about."

I held out the orders and he took them unbelievingly. He stared, blinked, read again; then he looked up at me. They say Russians are very emotional; perhaps that is why his eyes seemed dark and almost wet.

His voice was strained. "We are Judases, you and I," he choked. "Those poor animals!"

74

X

JUDASES WE PERHAPS WERE, but the animals didn't seem to mind. We drew a full complement for *Weems:* three dogs, including Josie, two small apes, and a seal. The seal was not physically present—she stayed in the pool up in the Project area; but if *Weems* or anything like *Weems* ever put to sea, she would go along.

On an actual strike it wouldn't be both the dogs and the apes, but one group or the other; in our dry run one of our principal missions was to find out which could operate a submarine better. The apes had manual dexterity, which was helpful; but in the sheaf of preliminary studies Lineback threw at me it turned out that the dogs had more tolerance for low-level radioactivity, which might be more important. The reactor was not completely bare, of course; it still had a stripping of some light metal around it, filtering out gamma radiation and some of the other by-products. But neutrons, for instance, floated right through! With the light sheathing, being within range of the reactor meant slow, not sudden, death. And, of course, for the first part of the time the subject was dying of radiation poisoning he wouldn't know it; being an animal, he wouldn't ever know it, until he dropped dead—but that might take weeks.

The seal was somebody's bright idea, and I could see that she might be the most useful of all. Imagine a seal, trained to follow orders, carrying a leechbomb to a cruising Caodai ship. It wasn't that they couldn't detect her—but supposing they did detect her, what would they do about it? They weren't going to blow every fish, whale and dolphin that came within range of their sonars out of the water, and our seal would look like any other seal, except for what she carried. It was extremely doubtful that they could recognize what she carried in time to do them much good.

Working with the seal, in fact, was child's play. All we

75

had to do was to run through enough of a vocabulary to explain to her that if she swam to the object that was shown to her and pushed the big metal disk she would get a fish—and prove it to her with a couple of fish.

She would be one surprised seal when she pushed the big metal disk in an actual operation.

Semyon got a fit of the giggles every time he saw me trying to take a shower with my little aluminum helmet on my head. On Lineback's orders, I kept my mouth shut about what it was for; but as Lineback had promised, they began cropping up all over the base before long. Kedrick was the second man to turn up with one; then three or four of the other officers, including the WAVEs; then the enlisted personnel—apparently on the principle that they were comparatively expendable. My own WAVE appeared at the keyboard of the computer one morning with a feminine-styled model perched on the back of her head. It was smaller than mine—apparently a later issue—which, considering that mine was no more than three or four days old, indicated a pretty high priority in project development. Evidently the burns were causing more trouble than the newspapers reported.

And by then, of course, the reason for the helmets was an open secret. Semyon's feelings were hurt. "I have not enough brain, then?" he asked bitingly. "The Orientals cannot vector in the little brain of Semyon Timiyazev, the son of a disciple of Pavlov? Hah!" He was moody about it for days, until we got a shipment of helmets of a new size and shape. *Then* he was utterly crushed: The new helmets were for our dogs!

I tried to explain to him that it was a matter of ESP sensitivity, not intellect; that our work with the dogs might have made them susceptible. But you cannot tell a Russian anything once he gets an idea fixed in his brain; and for some little time after that Semyon was of no use to Project Mako; all he could do was stare at the dogs and sigh.

But the work proceeded.

I pushed myself pretty hard, because along about the

76

time I got my first command I got a letter from the Red Cross. "Lieutenant Miller," they said, "we regret to inform you in answer to your request of 28 June that we are unable to establish contact with Elsie NMI Miller, Signalman 2/C, last known to be interned at AORD S-14, Zanzibar, due to current security restrictions in force. Application has been made for permission for a Red Cross representative to visit her for the purpose of ascertaining her welfare, in line with your request. However, we must inform you that there is a backlog in excess of fourteen hundred such applications. None have been granted."

So I pushed myself hard, and the animals and Semyon harder still.

The hull of the *Weems* began to smell a little bit like an old goat barn. "Trained, these animals," Semyon complained bitterly. "They are not even house-broken."

But that had little to do with their military occupational specialty. The chimpanzees were named Clara and Kay, both females, both young and friendly; they caught on to what we wanted of them quickly enough. It was a spectacular sight to see Semyon, vocabulary sheets in his hand, chattering and posturing at the apes, but it got results. I found out very quickly that there wasn't any such thing as a conversation with an ape. You could stand there and tell it the chimpanzee symbols for, "Loud noise. Hurry. Grab-*that*-thing. Pull," and it would merely look at you, head cocked far over on one side, brown ape eyes staring vacantly. And then it would scratch and scamper away. But then the crash-dive bell would sound, and Clara or Kay would leap up from her flea hunt and jerk open the manual, main-tank valve as skillfully as any twenty-year submariner. I don't mean to say that they never talked back—often they would object and complain and tell us that they wanted a banana or a shiny ball or a handful of meal worms. But there was little consecutivity in their responses.

The dogs were another matter entirely. Their main problem was garrulousness; you would explain to them,

77

say, a complicated course-correction maneuver, and they would bark, growl and semaphor the whole thing back to you. And they wouldn't repeat it just once; they would tell you the whole procedure two or three times, and then come up and put their forepaws on your legs and mention a couple of the high spots, and tell you about the fire control drill they had done the day before, with emphasis on how High-Shiny-Lever was *not* the same as Little-Thick-Lever, even though both of them had to be pulled sharply outward. Semyon was astonished. "Oh that Mamushka should not see!" he moaned. "Observe, Logan! They chat like diplomat's wives!"

It was true enough; when we left them in a simulated abandon-ship, retreating to the whaleboat and communicating with the animals in *Weems* proper only through the telecom, they chattered at each other. Since a very large proportion of canine vocabulary is aromatic, that contributed to the soggy state of *Weems*'s interior. Fortunately, those sections of their vocabulary—though of paramount interest to the dogs—had nothing to do with ship handling, so it wasn't necessary for us to duplicate them.

The biggest hitch in communicating from the whaleboat was that we were living a lie, and we knew it. It was all very well to dry-run the animals from the whaleboat, in communication by means of the telecom, but in actual combat we would not be so fortunate. Water bars microwaves; communication is possible, but only by sonar beam, and that presents a real challenge to a telecom.

But not one which COMCARIB refused. Early one morning the engineers were back, ripping out all our communication equipment and replacing it with something complicated and new. Semyon and I sat on the shore, playing with Josie's puppies and waiting, and the whole business was installed in an hour.

The engineer from COMCARIB mopped his brow and explained it to us. "Oof," he said, sweating. "It's a sonar-vision installation, and Flag Section thinks it ought to do for whatever kind of lashup you guys have got here."

He looked puzzledly at Josie and at Semyon and shrugged, "Anyway, it'll give you a two-way picture. But not instantaneous; it's got a slow rate of scan, and you can transmit about one full image every two seconds. There's a little bell that rings when your picture is taken. The phosphors in the picture tube are——"

From there on it got deep, but I understood. Instead of radio waves, which the sea would stop, this thing beamed sound waves, which the sea carried beautifully; but because of the slow speed of sound waves, apparently, we were confined to transmitting a series of stills instead of a movie.

When I pounded it through Semyon's head, after the engineers had left, he glowered at me. "But the *essence*, Logan," he complained, "the *essence* of the vocabulary is *motion* and——"

I patted him on the head. "Back to the computers," I said, as kindly as I could.

Well, we worked it out, and if we didn't have perfect rapport with the animals, there were compensations—with practice they got almost good enough to shiphandle by themselves anyhow.

The image in the sonarvision screen wasn't terribly sharp, but by turning up the gain we got a patchy sort of vivid light-and-dark silhouette that looked awful to me, but which the dogs and apes had no trouble recognizing. The only thing was, they couldn't seem to grasp the notion that the picture of Semyon was the same as the person of Semyon; they would take orders from Semyon in person, but the semaphoring stills only puzzled them.

We ran picture recognition tests for two whole days, and Josie was the first of the dogs to begin to get the idea. I pointed to Semyon and announced his name; I pointed to the photo of Semyon the signal lab had made for us, as contrasty as the screen image, and named it, and Josie got up on her hind feet and leaped over to the photo and licked it. It was like winning the Battle of the Atlantic.

"Good girl," I said in English, because by the time we got the dogs they had already naturally acquired ten or twenty loan words, like any other reasonably intelligent mutt. And, in Dog: "Now. This one. Do."

It was a photo of a cow. Josie stared at it thoughtfully for a moment and then pronounced "Big——." Well, never mind what the Dog word for "cow" is. But she got it. I ran through a couple of dozen pictures, and she called every one; and when I came to a photo of her puppies she called each name and, barking the look-at-me symbol, rolled over on her back to display her swollen milk glands.

I took a break, scratching the back of Josie's neck and smoking a cigarette. She said the low, half-voice whine for "Bad smell" once, but only as a comment, not a reproof, and she nudged my cigarette case indulgently with her nose.

I picked it up and opened it. Elsie's picture was inside the lid, taken two years before. I started to tell Josie that this was my wife, but somehow it didn't seem right, translated into Dog, and I contented myself with showing her the picture. She looked at it a little dubiously, tongue lolling out, one paw on my knee.

I didn't think how odd that might look to anyone else until I heard Lineback's voice, scratchy with astonishment and scorn, from behind me saying: "What are you trying to do, Miller, make her jealous?"

Lineback went through *Weems* like a homing torpedo through a tube, and in that one half-hour inspection there wasn't a thing that Semyon and I had been doing that he didn't touch on. He was wearing a sardonic expression when he began, but by the time he completed his tour and watched us put the animals through a couple of simple paces his face was serious and friendly. "Lieutenant Miller, Lieutenant Timiyazev," he said, "well done. Now I've got a hard question for you. Do you think you can make this thing work in combat?"

Semyon swallowed audibly. I said quickly: "Certainly, sir."

Lineback looked at me thoughtfully. "You're pretty salty," he said, and I couldn't tell whether it was approbation or not. "Well, you may get the chance. You'll have orders tomorrow." He reached over to pat Sammy, our wirehair. Sammy glanced at Semyon, who told him:

"Boss. All right here."

Sammy whined. You could translate it as, "Well, if you say so"—and suffered Lineback to pat him. Lineback shook his head. "That business with your hands and the growl—you were talking to the pup?"

"That is correct, Commander," said Semyon proudly. "I translate it like so——"

"Never mind," said Lineback. "I don't know, it seems to me things were simpler before this thing got started." Sammy was acting ill at ease, so Lineback let him go. "Dogs usually like me," he said. "Been getting along with animals all my life. I suppose once they get in the habit of conversation with humans, it changes their attitudes a little."

"That is so," Semyon said eagerly. "One picks up a little of culture from the other; it is a phenomenon well known. You will find it in the papers of my mother, who worked with Pavlov."

"No doubt," said Lineback drily, and got up to look for his hat. I got up with him; he had left the hat at A-Hatch and——

"Sammy!" I yelled. The terrier, surprised in the act, looked around at me and whined, and reluctantly lowered his leg. I rescued the commander's hat, just in the nick of time.

Commander Lineback, I will say for him, rose to the occasion. He looked at me for a speculative moment, then smiled slightly. "I see," he said impassively. "Well, you won't have to translate that for me. Good day, gentlemen."

And he left, leaving Semyon and me staring at each other in horror and relief.

XI

So WE FOUND ourselves on orders. It wasn't Lineback who handed us the orders. It was a special courier-officer from a higher command, and it wasn't even COMCARIB that wrote them, though it had COMCARIB's humble and instant endorsement. But the orders were signed "By command of COMINCH" himself, and the courier was a full commander of the Line.

Semyon was awed. "It is big, Logan," he said portentously. "Did you observe? He shares your tastes in hats."

"I observed," I said. The commander had worn the aluminum skullcap under his regulation dress cap, a style which was becoming fashionable. We broke the seal on our orders, and read them hurriedly. They explained very little, only that we were detached from Project Mako as of 0800 the next morning, and were to proceed without delay to a port on the Florida Gulf coast for assignment. That was all my orders said. Semyon's had one extra paragraph—directing him to bring with him certain "experimental animals covered by References COMINCH KT-41-611-MAKO and COMINCH KJA-41-1845-MAKO, specifically one (1) bitch, two (2) dogs, two (2) apes, small, female, and one (1) seal.

The orders were headed MOST SECRET, and consequently it was inevitable that everyone we saw on Project Mako stopped us to say good-by. We reported in to Commander Lineback, who made the most sensible suggestion of the day. "Go out," he said, "and get drunk. It may be a long wait for the next time."

So we headed off base and wound up in the Passion Pit—but not, this time, without shots of our own. When the waiter finally made it to our table, Semyon ordered ginger ale and I ordered chicken broth setups, and we got set to enjoy the floor show.

The stripper went through the whole act without interruption, and I must say it was worth it. She was a lovely woman, golden-haired, blue-eyed, tall and shapely; she had a figure that no woman deserved; and it was incontrovertibly natural, she went to some trouble to prove it. Because Semyon made a point of those things, we were seated at ringside, and he invited her to our table when she paused right in front of us near the end of her number. I was surprised she didn't have us thrown out. I was even more surprised when, five minutes after she made her last bow, she showed up at our table.

"Lovely," said Semyon sentimentally, looking at her costume. It was civilian clothing, rare enough on a young girl; you could see the fall-away zippers and clippers that marked it as part of her professional wardrobe. "I have not seen many such dresses in your country. May we offer you a drink?" He reached for his flask as I reached for my case; we both held them out at the same time.

"Thanks," she said with a warm smile. "I'll pop, please?" Semyon shook his head in sad resignation.

"Mad," he said. "However—waiter!"

The waiter came over and took our orders—the same setups for Semyon and myself, beef bouillon for the girl. "My name," she said, "is——"

"Caresse O'Nuit," said Semyon promptly. "I have seen the billboards."

"But my *name*," she said, "is Nina Merriam, Ensign, USWNR."

"Of course," Semyon said humbly. "I am sorry, Nina. It is a much more lovely name."

"Which is?"

"Nina Merriam is."

"Is it?" She thought about it. "No, I think you're wrong," she decided. "But it's my real name, so let's use it, shall we?"

Semyon said: "I would use any name that would bring you to me."

She looked at him. "Down, boy," said Nina Merriam.

"Chicken broth," said the waiter, arriving. "Ginger ale. And here's your beef bouillon, Nina. Better take it easy; the old man's out back."

"Don't worry about me," said Nina, and looked at me expectantly. I took out the case again and offered her her choice. She hesitated, then picked a flat green one.

"They're doubles," I warned her.

"So we'll live a little." She popped the pastille into her mouth and swallowed it expertly, dry. She sat for a moment before she took the first spoonful of the chaser. "Good stuff," she said.

I was feeling my first one by then; but, after all, as Commander Lineback had said it might be a long time before we had another chance to hoist a few. I took a double too—but unlike sweet, blonde, young Nina Merriam, I had to wash it down with half the chicken broth.

They say that you don't really get any physical kick out of popping for at least half an hour—it takes that long for the build-up. But I swear I get a tingle as soon as it slides down my throat. Call it psychological and maybe it is; but I can feel my temperature go up, I can see things begin to take on that lovely, fuzzy, dreamy look, I can feel that funny hot tingle go through my body.

Semyon, of course, disapproves. He sat glumly sipping his Scotch and ginger ale and watched us. "Filthy custom," he grumbled. "Thank heaven is not found in Russia."

"They used to say the same thing about alcohol," I said dreamily. " 'S just a poison, alcohol. Why would anybody want to poison himself?"

"Be easy on him, Lieutenant," Nina broke in, pushing away the balance of her chaser. "I kind of wish I could get as big a charge out of liquor as I do out of bios. I'm getting fat as a pig on the chasers."

"Oh, no, no," said Semyon at once, dropping the whole discussion. "I have seen many pigs, Nina Merriam. Truly, there was none of them who was not much, much fatter than you."

"Thanks."

"You are welcome," said Semyon proudly. "You have in no respect a figure like a pig's. Observe that in hog, the middle section bulges out like watermelon. Your mid-

84

dle section is slim—two-hands slim, I estimate. Utterly unlike pig. I have covered waist; now I proceed upward. Pig——"

"No you don't," said the girl. "Forget about the pigs."

"Of course," said Semyon. "But pig——"

"I think pigs are dirty animals," said the girl definitively.

Semyon giggled and slopped more Scotch into his glass. "So you say of pig," he observed. "And pig says of you ——" And he told her, in Pig, what pigs called humans. It was the same term as they used for portions of their swill; it sounded like a hay fever patient blowing his nose.

The girl looked suddenly interested. "I didn't know you were a farmer," she said.

"Farmer? Timiyazev is no farmer! Logan here and I we——"

"Semyon! Shut up!" I had been half asleep in my chair, dreamily listening to them, thinking how far away and curious everything was; but Semyon brought me to with a bang.

He said angrily, "Do not shut me up, Logan! I was not going to speak of Project Mako!"

"You better not," I told him, and went back to examining my own sensations. I was beginning to see things through a haze. I looked down at the floor, where a cigarette was smoldering far, far away; it reminded me to take a drag on my own cigarette, and when I raised my fingers to my lips there was no cigarette in them. It posed an interesting problem. Cigarettes appeared from nowhere on the floor, cigarettes disappeared from my hands; it was all incomprehensible and suspicious. Was it possible that the Caodais were up to tricks with my cigarettes? I thought it over, and rejected the possibility. The pacifists, yes; that might be it. But it couldn't be the Caodais, because they were too far away. It had to be pacifists. However, I had a plan to outwit them; it involved bending over and picking up the cigarette on the floor. It took a little thinking, but it was workable: It would restore the balance.

85

While I was working out the details, Nina Merriam said, "How about another round?" The waiter appeared and disappeared, and new setups were on the table.

"Logan," Semyon was saying insistently. "Logan, why don't you answer me?"

"What is it that you would like an answer to?" I asked him carefully.

"I asked you if I might tell Nina about Josie's puppies."

I touched my finger tips together. "I see," I said. "You want to know if you can tell Nina about Josie's puppies."

"That's right."

"Don't interrupt me, Semyon. I'm thinking." I closed my eyes to concentrate. The problem had many ramifications, and I couldn't help wondering how Semyon had got onto that subject in the first place. Lineback would throw a tizzy if he even knew that Semyon had so much as admitted he'd ever *seen* a dog. But Lineback, of course

——

"Logan!" Semyon sounded angry. "Wake up!"

I opened my eyes and smiled at him forgivingly.

"Well?" he demanded. "What is your verdict?"

"This is my verdict," I announced. I paused to frame the thing in exactly the right words. I was feeling a little woozy from the double shots, there was no denying it. Not only was I flushing hot all over, but I could feel my skin getting dry and my pulse thudding; it was time to take it easy for a while. I said carefully: "You can't tell her about the puppies. You can tell her about Josie herself, all right; but you mustn't mention talking to her, or the *Weems*."

He shook his head disgustedly. "Curse this security," he said.

"Don't say anything about our shipping orders either," I warned him.

"Of course not, Logan! Do you think I am a loosetongue? Well, Nina, I cannot discuss the puppies, so do not ask me. I won't do it."

I nodded approvingly, and closed my eyes to listen better.

This time it was the girl who said, with a touch of irritation, "Wake up, Lieutenant Miller. The chaser's getting cold."

"Sorry," I mumbled, and found my case. She grabbed it, apparently under the impression that I was going to spill its contents. "No need to get excited," I protested.

She said, "You've only got one anthrax left. Maybe you'd better lay off for a while."

I sat up straight. "Help yourself," I said cordially. "Officer of the Line can mix his shots. Don't expect girl to do as much."

She took the flat green pastille and swallowed it, making a face as she sipped the lukewarm bouillon. I took one at random and popped it. "Hey!" she cried, but I already had it down and was choking on the chicken broth.

"You shouldn't have done that," Nina said worriedly. "Do you feel all right?"

"I feel ferfec— *per*fectly fine." It wasn't entirely true, and I avoided her eyes, not so much because they were accusing as because they were attached to her face, and her face was moving. I didn't want to look at any moving objects just then. I stared at the ceiling, waiting for the slight tremor inside me to go away.

It didn't. I took a deep breath and sat up straight—it seemed hard to stay erect for any length of time—and smiled at Semyon and the girl. "Dance, Miss Merriam?" I invited.

"There isn't any music," she pointed out.

But Semyon responded, even if the girl was a spoilsport. His eyes jerked open. "Dance!" he said. "Timiyazev will dance *lesgilka* for you?"

"Oh, no you won't," said Nina Merriam, and between us we got him back in his chair. I had had only one more shot than the girl, but I was frankly reeling and she seemed as fresh as a daisy. I don't know how women do it. She reminded me of my wife: Elsie and I had pub crawled three nights a week for half a year before we were married, and it was always I who began getting disorderly.

Semyon resisted only briefly; then he sat back, sprawled

87

in his chair, and smiled lovingly at us. "Good party, Logan," he said.

"The best," I said.

I sneaked a look at my watch; it was hard to make it out, and even harder to perform the necessary subtraction, but as near as I could figure it was two hours since I had taken my first shot. The anthrax colonies in my system were pretty well established; I had a fine building case of fever and approaching delirium. Any minute now the second layer of the pastille would dissolve and the antibiotics would take over, cleaning out the bacteria and sobering me up. It was about time, I thought fuzzily, computing the time to get back to base and the amount of sleep I would have before our transportation arrived the next morning.

And I completely forgot the trouble with mixing your shots. For the antibiotics are specifics; the cores that will sober up your case of anthrax in an hour don't touch pneumococcus or the others. I was in for a double-jointed hangover—still drunk on the second dose while I was being sobered up from the first. I didn't know it, and it was just as well.

But I knew it the next morning. Oh, yes.

XII

"Do what I do," I told Semyon, who was rubbernecking at the big ships in the wash. He glowered resentfully, but he followed orders.

We stepped into a submersible whaleboat and sat ourselves in the sternsheets while a couple of efficient seamen disposed of the crates containing the animals in the cargo space. They were almost all the baggage Semyon and I had between us; the orders had specified strip-ship condition. It meant battle stations; it meant the big-ship Navy and a combat mission; it meant, perhaps, getting somewhere near the east coast of Africa and Elsie.

We boarded *Monmouth*, a 40,000 ton carrier, by one of the three after gangways, and Semyon was so preoccupied watching the whaleboat carrying our animals to a forward gangway for loading that he almost forgot to salute the colors. I nudged him, and he looked at me blankly for a moment before he remembered our careful rehearsal. Josie and the apes were easier to train than Semyon Timiyazev.

Our quarters were small but comfortable; we shifted into dress blues and reported to the Executive Officer, and were sent immediately to see the Captain. I had almost forgotten such niceties of the naval service as the Captain's call. I would have felt like the wanderer coming home, except that I wasn't feeling much of anything except a queasiness in my stomach and a throbbing like *Monmouth*'s main-drive engines in my head. But I got through the interview with the Captain all right, and so did Semyon. Having a hangover is not, after all, the worst thing that can happen to a naval officer on his first day at a new ship; it tends to make you concentrate on what you are doing.

But as soon as we had a moment to ourselves, we headed for the sick bay and wheedled vitamin shots out of one of the surgeons. *He* thought it was very funny. They helped, but I did not enjoy the surgeon's prescription for "helping to re-establish the intestinal flora" which he claimed the antibiotics had pretty well knocked out. It was yogurt, and I forced it down, but I almost lost it again when Semyon cried delightedly; "*Schav!* Please, Doctor—me too," and proceeded to swallow a pint of the stuff.

All in all, we were in pretty good shape for the briefing at 900 hrs. the next morning, except for Semyon's nagging worry about his beloved dogs. "Josie, of course," he told me fretfully. "They understand Josie, she is on the orders. And Sammy is all right, and the apes. But the little puppies, Logan, will they be all right? No orders for them, you know."

I chased him down to the whaleboat level to look them over.

Before sunrise we got under way. *Monmouth* slipped lines and stood out into the channel—on the surface, since Caodai radar didn't matter on our initial course in the Gulf. I was on deck in officer's country as we sailed, feeling useless, with reason. I had no part in the complicated task of getting a war vessel on course.

Faint dawn light was coming up behind us. *Monmouth* blinkered good-by to the harbor monitor through a gentle drizzle, and then the hailer gave all of us idlers the warning, *Stand by to submerge.* I found a spot out of the traffic lanes, near a running port; and I watched through the glass as the deck parties stripped and stowed the outboard gear. They did their job and disappeared in well under sixty seconds. *Monmouth* was a taut ship.

There was a hoot and jangling of bells, and *Monmouth* slid downward into the water. Green and blue waves bubbled up over my port; turned brackish gray; and then there was nothing at all to see, nothing but a faint sourceless light through the water outside.

I went to the briefing in a thoughtful mood, and was astonished at the number of officers there—nearly sixty.

The ship's Executive Officer rapped his knuckles against the standing microphone and called us to attention.

He looked at us queerly for a moment before he spoke. Then he waved a red-sealed envelope and said:

"Welcome aboard, gentlemen. You've all got quarters and you all know you're on a crash-priority mission, and half of you have been haunting my office ever since we got under way. Well, I couldn't tell you anything. I've been in this Navy for forty-six years, and I've heard of sealed orders, and I always thought they were something you read about in books." He slapped the envelope against the mike, and the amplified *thud* rolled around the room. "That's what we got here. Sealed orders. In—" he glanced at his watch—"in one minute the Captain's going to be opening his copy of these, and then we'll all know what we're up to. Until then, hold your breath."

He rocked back on his heels, calmly observing his watch. Then he leaned forward again, and I guess we all really did hold our breaths. He said: "I forgot to tell you, those of you that don't know it already, that Captain's Calls are suspended for the time being, so don't bother me for appointments."

There was a groan from the sixty of us, and he said: "All right, gentlemen. Here it is." And he stripped the seals off the envelope and began to read.

It was a crash-priority mission, all right. Even the weary old Exec stood straighter and seemed to come alive as he read the formal phrases from the orders.

It was—the Glotch—though that wasn't what the orders called it. Intelligence had come up with the conclusion that the Caodai Headquarters for the new weapon was not on the interdicted mainland, but on the island of Madagascar. Our sortie was to make reconnaissance, to find out what was there—and, if possible, to pulverize it.

"Target Gamma." That's what the orders called it— a point fixed with grid markings on a map. Something was there, something which the Caodais were trying as ably as they could to hide. We were going to take a look.

91

The Exec finished reading the orders, and folded the sheet.

"Specific assignments will be given out later, by sections," he said after a moment. "Gentlemen, this has been as much of a surprise to me as to you, as I mentioned earlier. But I suppose we all had an idea that it might have something to do with the Caodai weapon.

"I only want to add one thing to what you've just heard. It's no secret that the Cow-dyes have been hitting us pretty hard. Well, it's been worse than you think. Worse than we can stand, in fact." He licked his lips. "Gentlemen, you're in for some rough times, and only a fool would try to tell you that you're all going to come through them alive. But keep this in mind: This is for keeps. I have it from the Captain. If this doesn't work, the JCS's next recommendation to the President will be a declaration of war. It's as serious as that.

"We've got to come through. Or else it means the satellite bombs for everybody."

That was that; we were dismissed. We left the briefing room silently, all of us too busy thinking about what the Exec had said and its implications to talk.

But we were not all thinking of the same implications. I raced from the briefing room to the chartroom, to confirm what I already knew but could hardly believe.

Our target was Madagascar, a long, fat island hanging off the east coast of Africa. And next above it, inches away on the map, another island——

Zanzibar!

And Zanzibar meant Elsie.

Semyon came chortling to me: "At last we are equals! I have been promoted, I am now considered as valuable as you and the animals!" He displayed what had just been issued to him, an aluminum helmet, protection against the Glotch. The whole ship was being fitted with them.

"We're late," I growled at him, and tugged him away to our special section briefing. I had been on edge ever

92

since I had found out how close I was coming to AORD S-14, where my wife was eking out her days in the monotony of a prison camp. Incredible that I could come that close to her and not see her! But impossible that I could do anything else! For all of my months on *Spruance* I had been praying for just such a strike; and now that it was within grasp, it was worse than anything I could have imagined. *So near*, I said to myself—and for the first time understood how powerful the ragged, hackneyed clichés of speech had to be to survive so long—*so near and yet so far*.

Our special section briefing was very exclusive—the briefing officer, Semyon, and me. He began without preamble: "There will be three waves against Target Gamma, and you are in Wave One. There will be three groups in Wave One: Group A, air reconnaissance. That's radar-proof gliders, launched at sea, with infrared scanners and so on. Group B is intelligence officers—they're Oriental nationals, mostly from Hawaii, I think, for infiltration. Group C is animal penetration—that's you."

He closed his Plans book with a snap and said: "Your mission is to get your animals as close to Target Gamma as you can and get them back. You will spend the next seven days rehearsing them; they will have to learn to use small cameras, which they will carry around their necks, and they will take pictures of *everything* in the area. You two are expendable, but the animals are not—until they've got the pictures, anyway."

I glanced at Semyon—the briefing officer had just sunk *Weems*, and my visions of my first combat command. "How are we supposed to get the animals back if we're expendable?"

"We'll establish a rendezvous point where they can be picked up. Frankly, I think you two will get caught. Maybe it will be even better if you *do* get caught," he added callously, "because it'll give the Caodais something to do. You—" he nodded at Semyon "—may get by; you'll have cover papers as a Ukrainian neo-Bolshevik refugee, of which Intelligence thinks there is a small colony on

Madagascar. But you—" that was me "—are going to have to just stay out of sight. Oh, we'll color up your skin and give you what looks like a prosthetic arm, and hope you may pass for a disabled Caodai veteran. But don't count on it. The dogs, remember—they're what's important. Unless there's been a worse security leak than we have any reason to believe, the Cow-dyes won't be on to the animal bit."

That was about all there was to it. Going back to our quarters I thought of the endless days on *Weems*, training the animals to operate a ship. Was it all camouflage? Were the guiding geniuses behind Project Mako trying to throw dust in the eyes of the Caodais, in case they penetrated our security?

Or was it merely that things had got tight, and whatever long-range plans COMINCH had for Project Mako had to be scrapped in favor of this all-or-nothing effort against Target Gamma?

Still, I thought, looking through the portholes at absolutely nothing—we were fathoms down and running lightless—maybe the prospects weren't so bad after all. Maybe the expendable unit in this operation—myself—might actually enjoy being expended.

It was all pretty far-fetched, I admitted to myself, but consider: If the Caodais nabbed me, say, the chances were that they would not shoot me out of hand. True, I would be a spy, and they certainly weren't going to pat me on the back and send me home with an ice-cream cone in one hand and a red balloon in the other.

But we weren't at war. *We* didn't shoot Caodai spies. We arrested them, and tried them, and threw them in jail or in concentration camps.

But would that be so bad—assuming, I mean, that the Caodais were as humane as we? Maybe the punishment would be something like imprisonment in a PW camp. And maybe, just maybe (but still, how conveniently close at hand it was!), the PW camp would be AORD S-14, the one which held the heart and soul of all the world . . .

We were supercargo, all of us expendables of the three

94

waves, and we didn't have much to do except keep out of the way.

Semyon, grown queerly moody, spent most of his time slumped over a chessboard in our wardroom. I offered to play a game with him, and his refusal was a masterpiece of tact. Even tact didn't get him out of a game with the duty officer late one night, and Semyon trounced him so economically that I realized why he hadn't been greatly interested in playing against me.

I tried to make friends with some of the ship's officers, but they looked on us with something of the air Chicago's stockyard workers have toward the cattle. They didn't *want* to make friends. I did manage to get into a few bridge games in the ship's wardroom, but always with the feeling of being an interloper. And the ship's officers, for that matter, struck me as an eccentric lot, far below the standards of *Spruance*. The only one I cottoned to at all was a gunnery officer named Rooie, like myself a former scout-torp pilot on a *Spruance*-class cruiser, now on limited duty because of injuries which accounted for some of the three rows of ribbons on his chest. He was salty and amiable; but unfortunately the other officers of his duty section disliked me on sight. For a few days it was bearable, because they urgently needed a fourth for bridge. But after we went down five tricks, doubled and redoubled, after I had started with the Pratt convention (opening two-bid to show a void in a suit), my partner threw his cards on the floor. He was an ensign named Winnington, a beefy young redhead; and what he said about my bridge playing was bad enough, but what he said about me personally made it impossible to stay in the room.

So it all worked out for the best. Semyon and I spent tedious hours with Josie and Sammy, while the chimps asked ridiculous questions and the puppies got in the way; and they were all ready for the big performance. Heaven knows what sense they made out of the answers we gave to their "Whys"; but they knew their jobs.

From Florida we swept grandly south and east, as our course was lined out day by day in the chartroom. At 40 knots—not our best speed, but the one which made the least noise and fuss to alert Caodai sonars—we were clipping off nearly a thousand miles a day.

Each night we surfaced briefly to let the navigators obtain a fix, and for a few moments each time, half a dozen lucky souls were permitted out on the weather deck, perhaps to see the stars. But not me.

For eleven days I counted my fingers and thumbs, while we went from the Caribbean through the South Atlantic, and into the broad curve that grazed the Antarctic Ocean itself south of Good Hope. And then we were creeping up the eastern flank of Africa—slow and wary.

These were interdicted waters. If we were spotted here, we were dead; at the best, we would have to abort and run. Our orders were to avoid engagement unless it was forced on us, but there was a pretty fair chance that we might have no choice. Consequently the fire control stations were double manned around the clock, and we crept under the thermoplane, in the dense Antarctic Deep water, with our fingers crossed. It was dead reckoning now; the navigators had only the fragmentary charts of submarine configurations to help them get a fix; surfacing, even for a moment, was out of the question.

The strain was beginning to tell on the ship's crew.

I looked in on Lieutenant Rooie's wardroom, and it was like the condemned row in the death house. Rooie was there, watching a canned TV program in a film viewer, and when I tapped him on the shoulder he jumped. "Oh, Miller," he said, but his eyes were haunted and it was a moment before he smiled. "How are you?" He switched off the film viewer. "I don't know what the blasted thing is about, anyhow. Want some coffee?"

He signaled the mess attendant without waiting for me to answer. She was an enlisted WAVE, rather attractive looking from the rear; I didn't get a good look at her face as she went out for our coffee.

96

Winnington appeared from behind a bookshelf. "Hello," he said, a little stiffly.

"Hi." If he wanted to forget the fracas at the card table, I was willing. We all sat down and talked about nothing in particular. They were eager to talk, even Winnington. It is an ugly companion, the knowledge that at any time some wandering Caodai sonar beam may bounce off your ship's hull and lead a torpedo to you.

"Your coffee, sir." Winnington took a cup, and the girl turned to me. She was attractive from the front, too; only a Seaman 2/c, but young and fresh looking. She wore no makeup, but——

But I had seen her before.

I had seen her before, and then she had worn quite a lot of makeup—makeup and little else!

"Nina Merriam!" I said. There was no doubt in my mind; the last time I had seen her, her hair had been a different color; but it was the same girl—the ensign stripper from the Passion Pit. I couldn't believe it, but I couldn't doubt it. She was a spy!

I stood up so fast that I kicked my chair over backward. "What the devil are you doing here?" I bellowed at her. Rooie and Winnington were asking startled questions, and I filled them in. Their reaction was sharper than mine.

"Spy!" gasped Rooie. "Miller, you've caught yourself a spy! Look at her—American as you and me, selling out to those lousy, stinking——"

We took her at quick-march down to the ship's Exeutive Officer's quarters, leaving Winnington gaping foolishly after us. There was an armed guard at his door. I told him: "Watch her. She's probably a spy. Hold her here while we talk to the Exec."

The girl said sharply, "I'm not a spy!" But what else would she say? Rooie and I pushed our way into the Exec's office, careless of shipboard protocol, and blurted out our story.

We must have sounded like idiots, but nothing ruffled the Exec. He'd said he had been in the Navy forty-six years; I believed every year of it. He stared at us thoughtfully, and lit a cigarette.

"A spy, you say." He puffed on the cigarette in an infuriatingly meditative manner. He was past retirement age, the kind of grizzled old three-striper who keeps passing his fitness tests out of spite, refusing to be put out to pasture. And he kept looking at us.

"Sir," burst out Rooie, "she's right in your anteroom. Why don't you——"

He stopped—just barely in time. Thunderclouds were gathering over the Exec. Well, after all—he was the administrative officer for the ship of the Line, and Rooie was a very junior lieutenant. But the explosion looked like it was going to be a beaut.

It probably would have been, if we had heard it.

But we didn't. The loud-hailers in the passageway cut it off. They rattled with the klaxon ship's alarm, and then the voice from the bridge blared!

"Attention on deck! Attention on deck! Bandits in fleet strength detected on intersecting course. Condition Crash Red! Battle stations all. Repeat, Condition Crash Red!"

XIII

THE LIEUTENANT didn't even wait to say good-by; he was out of that place and on his way to his battle station before the klaxon had stopped blaring. The Exec was a moment slower, but not because he was paying any attention to us. He bellowed something into his intercom, listened for a second, bellowed again, and was gone. Even the guard and the Exec's secretary were gone; there was no one left but the girl and me.

She said urgently: "Let me go, Lieutenant! You've got this all wrong. I've got to get out of here and——"

I said: "Shut up!" I was feeling jittery. General Quarters is a powerful voice of command. I had no battle station on *Monmouth*; I was supercargo, as useless in an engagement and as undesirable as the wardroom silver the old surface ships used to jettison before a fight. But I didn't want to be useless; I wanted to respond to the alarm, and all I could do was stay here and look ugly at a frail young girl. Bandits in fleet strength! It wasn't even a wanderer on picket duty or a cruising raider that we might hope to swamp before it could transmit a signal. It meant fleet action if they spotted us—and we were big enough for anybody to spot.

I felt the angle of the deck change, and, simultaneously, a slowing in the throb of the screws. I could see, in my mind, just what was happening: We were reballasting our tanks, tipping our diving fins, slowing our propellers to a gentle wash as we headed for the bottom. Under a good thick blanket of the dense, cold Antarctic Deep water we might not be spotted. Sonar echoes took odd bounces off the interfaces between layers of water of differing densities; and of all the water in the earth's oceans, Antarctic Deep made the sharpest, cleanest interface. That much, at least, was good. . . .

The girl was saying: "I tell you one more time, Lieutenant! Get out of my way. That's a direct order!"

99

"What?" I stared at her. I was between her and the door, and I was going to stay there. It would have been nice if I had had a weapon; I felt a little foolish, standing there with my bare hands hanging at my sides; but of course I shouldn't really need any more than bare hands to subdue a little hundred-and-five pound girl.

I said: "I'd appreciate it if you'd shut up until the Exec gets back. But you're not leaving here, understand that."

"You bloody fool!" she raged. "Don't you even listen to me? I'm not a Cow-dye, you idiot; I'm Nina Willette of Navy Intelligence and you're keeping me from the most important job I've ever done!" She took a deep breath and fought for control of herself. She was, all at once, superbly beautiful as she stood glaring at me, her shoulders thrown back, her breasts lifted, her eyes filled with fury, and I suppose she knew it very well. They are actors by trade, these cloak and dagger people; how was a simple Line officer like myself to know whether she was telling the truth or not? She said, with an effort: "Look, Lieutenant, I'll explain it to you. I'm Counter-Intelligence; I was on security duty when I was a stripper at Boca Raton; I'm on security duty now. There are pacifists in *Monmouth's* complement, Miller! Do you know what that means? Right now we're at battle stations; this is the time when I ought to be out on the prowl, making sure everybody's at his station, looking for trouble before it starts—and I'm here, waiting for a fat-headed j.g. to make up his mind to let me go. Move, boy! Get out of my way!"

"Good try," I said, but I was shaken. "Stay where you are."

Well, she was some kind of spy or counter-spy, but she was only a girl, and a small one and a young one at that. All of a sudden her eyes filled with tears. She sobbed and leaned blindly forward; instinctively I reached out to help her. She clung to me, weeping, and it was like holding a fragrant, sad flower. I hadn't known that enlisted women used perfume; I felt odd stirrings in my

100

middle, and suddenly the Exec and the encroaching Cao-dais seemed very remote, and I found myself patting her head and saying soothing things——

And then the roof fell in.

I came to with a lump behind my right ear, and there was no one in the Exec's office but me. Nina whatever-her-name-was was gone. Lord knows what she hit me with; but it was nothing to what the Exec hit me with when he came back for a brief racing second and found me standing dopily in the middle of the floor. I don't suppose he said more than twenty words to me, but every one of them dug deep under the skin and festered.

It seems that she was, indeed, Naval Intelligence. And a full Commander at that.

I saluted empty air; he was gone already. It seemed like a good place to be out of, so I left. In any case, even though I didn't have a real battle station there was a place where I was supposed to be. Semyon and I had been assigned a whaleboat, deep in the lower decks of the carrier, far below even the aircraft hangars, below the engineering sections, in the steel belly of the ship, surrounded by jet fuel for the aircraft and diesel oil for the torps and auxiliaries. It was where the animals were kept, for the whaleboat would be our assault vessel for the landing on Madagascar—if we ever got that far. And it was where I was supposed to be in any action.

I headed for it through the roaring tumult of a capital ship at general quarters. There was plenty of noise aboard the *Monmouth* just then, but it was mostly vocal—the racket of the loud-hailers, the sharp orders of the officers with their working parties, the rattle of sighting orders as I passed the fire control compartments. But the engines were a gentle whisper, barely enough to maintain steerage way. For human voices would not penetrate the ship's hull to give us away to the enemies around us in the dense, chill water draining off the Antarctic ice pack; but the sounds of our screws most surely would. We were well into the Indian Ocean, surrounded by Caodai Africa,

Caodai Asia and the inhospitable ice; the Caodais thought of it as their private lake, as we the Caribbean, and with just as much reason. Even if the sighted Caodai vessels missed us, there would be others . . .

Of course, we did have the curtain of the thermoplane over our heads, and that was a help. But it was as helpful to the Caodais now as to us. I was sympathizing with the men at the sonar stations, pinging into the dark deeps, charting and weighing the echoes that came back. There would be a vague splash of light in the sonar screen, warped by distance, almost obliterated by the thermoplane. Was it a blue whale, a school of fish—or a Caodai sub? Our real advantage was that we could fairly assume any sighting was a sub, whereas they might not expect to find us here.

Semyon was already in the whaleboat, of course. He was sitting with the puppies in his lap, talking nervously to Josie; he blinked at me as I slid in through the entrance hatch.

He scrambled to his feet, and then: "Oh," he said in relief, "it is you, Logan. I did not know but perhaps it was an admiral. In Krasnoye Army——"

"——There were no admirals," I finished for him. "Are the animals all right?"

"Oh," he said dourly, "they will perhaps survive if the rest of us do. Have you news, Logan? Are we to be in combat?"

"Can't you hear the squawk box?" It was rattling a repetition of what it had been saying, at intervals, ever since the first alarm: *Remain at stations. We have lost sonar contact, but the audic listening posts indicate the enemy still on course.* Which meant that we had stopped pinging the waters for fear of having them hear our own sonars; but our directional microphones had a fix on the Caodai screws, not muffled as ours were because, it appeared, they did not know we were around. It was good; if only they didn't close to a point where even the curtain between the dense, cold water and the bottom and the

102

lighter, warmer, saltier layers above no longer screened us from their sonars.

Semyon sat down and lifted the puppies into his lap. He clucked over them and petted them. "Always jumping up and down," he complained. "Is never a moment to sit, or to play chess, or merely to think. Ah, Irkutsk, if only I could see you once again! How precious the memory——"

His voice trailed off; he was staring past me at the entrance hatch. I turned; and there was Nina Willette-or-whatever. She was not alone. She had with her the surly officer named Winnington; and she also had a wide-mouthed, dangerous looking gun in her hand.

I said dazedly, "Lieuenant Timiyazev, Commander Willette."

Semyon pushed the puppies off his lap and stood up to give her a ramrod Red Army salute, hand twanging wide at the temple like the ancient Coldstream Guards. But he glanced at me inquiringly, all the same.

I started to explain, but Nina Willette cut me off. "Inside, Winnington," she said, and gestured with the gun. And to me: "Sorry to barge in like this, but I had to get him out of the way. They'd tear him to pieces back in the fire control room."

Winnington only looked even more sullen. He walked casually over to the navigator's desk, pushed Josie onto the floor and sat. "You've got no right to do this," he observed flatly.

"No right!" she blazed, but Semyon outblazed her.

"*Svoloch!*" he roared at Winnington. "Leave dog alone! She was not hurting you, the dog!" Josie whined her complaints; and then, as she caught the timbre of her boss's voice, barked threateningly: *Go away! Go away! Go away!*

Winnington looked more alarmed at Semyon and the dog than he had at Nina's gun. "Get these characters off me," he appealed to her.

"I ought to let the dog take a bite," she said sourly.

103

"But we'll save you for better things." She sat down, looking weary, and glanced at me. "Congratulations, Lieutenant," she said. "You almost loused things up, but not quite. I got to Winnington just as he was about to pull the trigger on the Caodais."

He said matter-of-factly: "I was setting up range and vectors. That's all. I wouldn't have fired without an order."

She laughed. "Of course not. And you're not a pacifist either, are you?"

"Pacifist?" I said, shocked; and Semyon blared:

"Patchifist? This one, a patchifist? Logan, leave me turn Josie loose on him! Is first patchifist I have ever seen!"

"Please," I begged him. "Tell me about it, Nina—Commander, I mean."

"Nina will do," she said wearily. "That's all there is to tell. I was assigned to keep an eye on him; he's been under surveillance for a long time. But he's smart. He didn't make a move—until it could be a big one. If I had been five seconds later he would have salvoed his whole battery at the Caodais; and they would have wiped us right out of the water ten minutes later."

Winnington laughed sharply, but he didn't say anything. He was watching Semyon, cradling Josie in his arms and murmuring to her in Dog, with what appeared to be genuine amusement.

A pacifist! I'd heard about them—I'd seen traces of their work, a newspaper report of a time bomb at the Caodai legation, an Army installation mysteriously ablaze—but as far as I knew I had never seen one in the flesh. And here was Winnington, my surly bridge partner of the wardroom, revealed as an authentic pacifist. It was like seeing a cobra emerging from a washstand drain—the essence of dangerous evil, where only familiar and safe things should be.

I started to question her, but the rattle of the loud-hailers in the passageway stopped me. There was a new tone to the bridge talker's voice: "Attention on deck! All hands

104

to Condition Baker! All hands to Condition Baker! Bandits past closest point of contact and holding steady on course." And then, humanly "They missed us!"

"So you see, patchifist," Semyon said nastily, "you have lost your chance!"

"Leave him alone," I told him. There was a tramping and talking in the passageways as the damage-control parties came up from the fuel tanks, where they had been waiting for possible Caodai hits, and almost certain cremation if one occurred. They looked hardly human in their anti-flash face paint and heavy hoods. Josie, spying them from the entrance hatch, barked like a rabid animal.

"Hush!" said Semyon to her, and repeated the order in Dog whine. I said to Nina Willette:

"Now what? Do you want me to escort you back to the Exec's office with this one?"

"Give us ten minutes," she said. "Let them cool off a little, I want him to get there alive. We pretty near had a lynching when I arrested him. He isn't popular with the ship's complement right now."

Winnington might not even have heard her; he was still watching Semyon trying to soothe the disturbed dogs, still with the air of amused detachment. He bent over casually to remove one of the puppies from his shoe, and Josie, the vigilant mother, sprang for him.

Semyon made a grab and caught her, yipping, by the tail, while the puppies clamored at him. "Fortune pulverize the fortune-pulverized beasts!" Semyon snarled. "Hush, now! Hush!" And he went on to bawl them out in Dog.

Nina said approvingly, "He barks like a native," and Semyon glowered at her briefly. But only briefly, because no mere human distraction could keep him from his animals.

"All right, all right!" he said, in a mock-furious motherly growl. "Semyon will tell you a story. Be calm! A nice story, I promise it. He had spoken in English, but the dogs, and even the seals behind their bars, reacted at

105

once. Apparently they recognized the word "story," which told me a little something I hadn't known before about why Semyon so frequently slipped back to the animal quarters for a few moments before he went to bed.

Winnington stared in disgusted unbelief and Nina almost exploded. Well, it was a mad sight: There were the animals, yapping with joy; there was Semyon, oblivious of us all; and there were Nina and Winnington, watching a full-grown fighting man tell bed-time stories to a brood of animals. It must have been funnier to them than it was to me, but it still was funny to me.

Semyon had a mixed audience. It was like tucking a six-year-old and a three-year-old into bed at the same time. One story will more or less do for both of them, but the differences in vocabulary mean you have to double up on the story as you go along—something like the facing Hebrew and English pages in the Holy Book they read from at the Christmas Feast of Lights. Semyon squatted down among the dogs, next to the seal pen; and then it was a steady stream of bark-whine-sniff-and-twitch, shiver-and-whine, grimace-and-growl. The animals were delighted; they followed the story with frantic absorption.

And Nina was delighted, too. After the first incredulous stare, she stuffed a handkerchief to her mouth and kept it there, eyes on Semyon, cheeks puffed out and pulsing. But she managed not to laugh out loud, which is more than I could say for Winnington.

But Semyon was oblivious. It was the longest monologue in any animal tongue I had ever heard, and I realized that it accounted for a lot in the comparative fluency Semyon had over me in talking with the dogs; it must have been splendid practice. I watched him admiringly as he improvised substitutes for words that did not exist, wagging the tail he didn't have, making the croupy barks that are Seal punctuation. When he finished, the animals applauded wildly.

And so did Nina. "Thank you very much," she said sincerely, regaining her self-control.

Semyon said suspiciously, "For what, thanks?"

"For telling us the story of Little Red Riding Hood. I wouldn't have missed it for the world."

He looked puzzled. "Oh, no, Commander," he said earnestly, "was not Riding Hood. How would that be tactful? Was Goldilocks and Three Bears, don't you see? Josie enjoys it very much, perhaps because of connotations of——" He stopped, indignant; Nina lost her self-control completely on that one. And when she laughed that broke me up.

But it didn't last. Nina stopped short and blinked at me. "What was that?" she asked shrilly.

But she knew the answer. I felt it too. The deck pulsed underneath us. A pause, and it pulsed again, as though a blue whale were nuzzling playfully up to *Monmouth* in our deeps.

But it was no whale, I knew. I had felt just that gentle pulsing on *Spruance*; I knew the feel of the recoil as a ship's main batteries loosed against an enemy.

Winnington grated triumphantly: "Caught me, did you? But maybe there was somebody you missed!"

Someone had salvoed a burst of at least a dozen missiles. If we had been hiding, we weren't hiding any more; beyond doubt, those missiles were laid on course at the fat and ignorant Caodais as they waddled blissfully away from us . . .

But they wouldn't be waddling any more.

XIV

IT WAS BAD. Worse than we figured.

While the four of us and the animals waited in the whaleboat, the loud-hailers roared orders and the ship lurched continually against the recoil of missiles leaving for Caodai targets. And then there was a shudder that was not a missile leaving the tubes. A Caodai torpedo had exploded against our deflection net, close enough to jar us all; and then another, and more, and one final one that was not against the net but against the hull of *Monmouth*; we were hit, and badly.

And even that was not the end.

Monmouth took six direct hits by my own count, standing helpless in the whaleboat. The ship was hurt. Our lights failed, and then went on again as the secondary circuits cut in; the secondaries failed, and our own whaleboat batteries lit the little cabin as I cut in the sealer switches. Outside in the passageways there was no power at all, at least in our deep laid section of the keelson; but from far away I could hear the rattle of the loud-hailers, and what they said was:

"All auxiliaries abandon ship. All auxiliaries abandon ship!"

And that was the beginning of eight long hours of death-in-life for the four of us.

We hugged the bottom; squatted there and waited.

Crippled *Monmouth* was still fighting. We could hear the distant explosions; but there wasn't anything we could do about it. Communication was impossible; the deeps were shuddering with explosions enough to drown out any call. To fight was out of the question: Our whaleboat had no armament, for the space for the missile rackets and projectile tubes had been pre-empted by the animal pens.

We squatted and waited.

There came a time when the noise of combat slacked

off and seemed more distant. I cut out the ruptured "eardrums" of our sound-ranging gear and tried to take a fix: There was still fighting, but it was drifting south of us and east.

Nina said over my shoulder, watching the indicator needles: "They're running for it. The Caodais are chasing them."

It seemed that way; but whatever *Monmouth* was up to, we had still only one choice: To wait. If we were spotted by any Caodai, even a corvette, we were done; but if we stayed dead and silent on the ocean floor, we had a prayer of a hope. We would be spotted, no doubt about it; but spotted as a hulk of metal, nothing more.

And the floor of the Indian Ocean just about there was rich in hulks of metal.

It was hard on us, but even harder on the animals. Josie was anxiously asking what the devil was going on, the puppies were alternately demanding food and whining for their box; the seals in their pens were barking worriedly. The process of learning had gone both ways. While we were picking up Dog and Seal, they were picking up human intonations. They could tell we were upset, and there is nothing in the world more likely to upset an animal than that knowledge. "Quiet, quiet," pleaded Semyon, in English and Dog and Seal. "You will drive me insane, you beasts." He pushed the puppies to the floor and called Josie to attend to them. "Dog," he said, but not to the animals; he was glowering at Winnington, silent against the hull of the whaleboat.

"Leave him alone," I said.

Semyon switched his glower to me. "Leave him alone, it is? But did he leave us alone? He sent us to the bottom, Logan! Filthy patchifist, he fired the guns!"

Winnington said morosely, "From here?"

"Hah," said Semyon. "No, not you, but your brother patchifist, whoever he was. For peace, you did it? Pig, how could it be for peace to make war?"

"For *ultimate* peace!" Winnington flared. "You think we *like* killing people, we peace men? You're an idiot;

109

you think that peace means sitting quiet and taking punishment, eh?" He was flushed and excited, taking a queer pleasure in the fact that we were all of us near death. "No!" he almost screamed. "That is not pacifism, that's stupidity! We must *fight* for peace, we must *destroy* the enemy. Kill everybody who might kill us—then, only then, we'll have peace!"

We finally hushed him.

At last, very cautiously, we rocked the whaleboat free of the mud and crept quietly to the thermoplane. We were no longer getting sounds of battle in the audic apparatus. Either the battle was over or out of range— or it was perhaps fairly close, but masked by the interface between the bottom water and the warmer waters above.

The thermographs showed us when we breached the interface. I cut the drive, cut the ventilator switches, cut every motor that could give out a sound, and we listened as hard as we could. The little torp began instantly to settle, but we had plenty of water under us, and the important thing was to be all ears, no sound, until we found out what was going on around us.

As the whaleboat lost forward speed the diving vanes ceased to bear us up and we slid downward, closer to the thermoplane we had just crossed. The auto-pilot began frantically manufacturing course corrections; it flipped the diving vanes and the rudders like a panicked barnyard hen, and when that produced no effect it began to beep complainingly. I snapped its cutoff switch and it was silent again; and we listened.

Nothing.

Nina said: "Do you think we ought to try the sonars?"

I shook my head and started the motors as we sank under the thermoplane again. "No sense looking for trouble. If somebody's playing possum close by, they'll hear us on their audic all right—but if we ping them, they won't even have to be close by." I locked in the auto-pilot. "Now what?" I asked.

110

It was a pregnant question. We had a long debate over what to do next.

But it could only have been decided one way, after all. Duty called. There was a Caodai installation on Madagascar, little more than three hundred miles away. Our mission was to survey it, if necessary to attempt to destroy it. We would carry out our mission—or die in the attempt.

Surprisingly, even Winnington agreed. "Very patriotic," he sneered. "But I'll go along. The sooner we wipe out those rats, the sooner the Peace Party can rule America."

"Very patriotic," Semyon agreed moodily. "Also quite wise, I think. Because—am I wrong, Logan?—we do not after all have a choice; we are ten thousand miles from home. And this little boat they gave us, its range is not more than a thousand . . ."

Madagascar was only three hundred miles away—but the island was almost a thousand miles long. It was touch-and-go whether we would make it.

Semyon swore gloomily, coaxing the power reserve along; we crept along the bottom, taking our position from sonar soundings and one daring midnight surfacing for a star fix. We made it.

We hovered in a muddy little estuary while Semyon talked lengthily to one of the seals. Then we coaxed the seal into the aft ejection tube. It wasn't necessary to blast him out with compressed air; he could swim free. He pilot-fished us up the little river as far as we dared go in the whaleboat, coming back to report and going forth to scout again. It was tedious, but reasonably safe.

We sent Semyon and Josie out to scout; it was night time, we were in a little cover, hidden by tangled growth. They were gone forever, and came back covered with mud.

"Is a terrible place, Logan," Semyon groaned. "I thought we would be captured many times. But—it is there."

"Target Gamma?"

111

"One presumes so." He sighed. "There is a small town, on this bank of the river; and perhaps two miles past it is a ring of labor camps. And in the center of the ring, something which is guarded. I did not myself see it, you understand; but Josie says it smells secret."

It was nearly dawn. Semyon was worn out, but Josie was frisky as a puppy. She tended her brood while we were talking, and demanded to be included in the party when we were through.

We left Semyon to watch over Winnington and the other animals; Nina, Josie and I made up the party that proposed to knock out the Caodai's secret weapon base.

A girl, a dog—and me. Nina, struggling into her Madagascan coolie outfit—slacks, sweater, floppy hat—saw my expression and laughed. "Cheer up, Miller," she said, "there's only about five million Caodais on the island—not bad odds."

I found myself grinning back at her. It was an odd thing; I couldn't help thinking about it, even with the approaching raid on my mind. Nina was an easy girl to get along with. It had been a long time since I had paid much attention to other girls. Why was it that now, with Elsie, comparatively speaking, almost within reach, I was suddenly noticing how pleasant and sweet and—and charming, I had to confess it, another girl was?

It wasn't a line of speculation I really wanted to follow to its end. I was glad when we slipped out of the upper hatch and climbed ashore to get started.

"*Alte-la, alte-la,*" grumbled the man in the yellow robe. "*Vous êtes bien pressée?*"

"Idiot," Nina muttered to me in English. "I *told* you to take it easy." She smiled appealingly at the priest and spoke to him in rapid-fire French. I could make out only part of it; we were freshly arrived from Tananarive and looking for work; could he direct us to a rooming house?

The Caodai shook his head. Without much interest he yawned and stretched and demanded our passports. That presented a problem, because Nina didn't have one. Semyon and I had been issued the best set of forged credentials Naval Intelligence could cook up; but no one had planned for Nina to be along. However, Nina's French could get by and mine couldn't; we were in trouble either way; we had decided to pass as man and wife and hope that one passport would do for both.

It did. Nina kept up a clamor of questions and comments while the priest was looking over the yellow card that identified me as an agricultural worker of French origin. There were plenty of them on Madagascar, hangovers from the colonial days and the overthrow that followed. The priest had evidently been up all night, and all he really wanted to do was collect a toll for crossing the footbridge; he tossed the document back at me and growled: "*Foutez le camp, tous les deux.*" We paid him and got along.

As soon as we were across the bridge into the town itself Nina turned on me: "Miller," she snapped, "if you can't relax we'll never get through. Walk *slowly*. You've been walking a long way; you're tired; you don't want to hop like a grasshopper and attract attention."

I transferred the cord tied to Josie's collar to my other hand. "Sure," I said. "What do we do, walk right through the town?"

"What else?" It was early morning, but already the streets were crowded. Most of the people moving about the narrow streets were Arab-African mixtures of one hue or another; but there was an admixture of Orientals and a handful of Europeans. More than half of the Orientals wore the yellow robes, blouse or shorts of the Caodais. But they were not alone; several priests we passed were obviously nearly pure African. Caodaism, like the Mohammedans before them, practiced a rigid sort of tolerance; there was no distinction in skin color or creed for them—if the man whose skin was in question was willing to embrace the Caodai revelations and, if necessary, join the Caodai armed forces.

And hundreds of millions throughout the Asian and African world had been more than willing.

The streets were not only narrow, they wound like worm holes in an apple. I had to consult Jose's superior sense of direction—bending and talking to her under pretense of loosening her collar—to keep us heading straight through the town. She was almost the only leashed dog in sight, and therefore attracted a little more attention than I liked. The Madagascan custom appeared to be to let dogs roam the streets, as unhampered and as privileged as a Benares bull.

Everyone, it appeared, spoke French. I remembered that the Caodais themselves had come from a section of the Indonesian peninsula once under French rule, and of course Madagascar had been French for nearly a century; but all the same it seemed odd to hear brown, black, tan and yellow faces conversing in the language I associated with bombed-out cities and Eastern finishing schools. . . .

"Softly," said Nina. "Keep your eyes on your lunch."

We were squatted beside the road as a company of Caodai infantry swung past. There was a sort of clearing in the vegetation, on the outskirts of the little town we had crossed; there were Oriental vendors of foods, and we were not the only ones who had paused there for a bite to eat. The Caodai soldiers paid no attention to any of us, being disciplined, eyes-front troops.

They passed. Nina left me for a moment with the dog, and talked briefly to one of the vendors. She came back with a handful of dried dates and two Coca-Colas and said:

"Security troops, I think. There are slave labor camps ahead. Does Josie recognize this road?"

I spoke to the dog; she growled back dubiously. "It smelled altogether different," I translated for Nina, "but she thinks it's the same place. It has something to do with daytime smells and nighttime smells."

Nina nodded. "It checks. Labor camps beyond the bend in the road, something big on the other side of them. According to the Coke man there's nothing to stop us

114

going right along the road—all the Caodai installations are off to one side, on the bank of the river."

It was high noon, or nearly, and most of the other pedestrians were disappearing down side roads and into shops and cafés. Nina and I conferred briefly, and followed their example. We struck out boldly down one of the little dirt paths toward the river, looking for a place to use as a base of operations. No one stopped us, no one paid any attention. I was expecting Caodai infantrymen to pounce out at us from behind every tree; I must have shown it, because Nina snapped: "I told you, Logan, relax. Nobody's going to bother us."

I suppose she was right. After all, we were not a platoon of commandoing marines, antiflash-painted, Tommy-gun-carrying, camouflage-helmeted. We were only a man and a woman and a dog; and if I had seen a party like ours anywhere in the United States I would scarcely have noticed the image that flashed on the retina of my eye. Except—

Come to think of it, I would have noticed such a party. I said curiously to Nina: "Notice anything about these people? Civilians! Outside of the Caodai priests, and the troops that marched by in the road—how many have you seen in uniform?"

She nodded thoughtfully. "Funny," she said. "A peculiar way to fight a war, I guess. You'd think they'd be as deep in this thing as we are, wouldn't you? Now look," she said, dismissing it, "how about holing up here and sending Josie in for a look?"

It was a good enough place, on the shore of the river, where we might appear to be resting and enjoying the view if anyone should come along. I talked to Josie long enough to make sure she understood. Josie was a patient dog, but she had very little comprehension of just what we superior humans were about, there on the banks of the Madagascan creek. She wasn't a stray mutt, and she didn't want to act like one; she complained that she had been told many times that it was impolite and inexcusable to eat out of garbage cans on nuzzle refuse piles for stray morsels—and yet that was what we were asking her to do now, to justify her wanderings. She was a well-brought-up bitch who had been taught to stay close to her home and master and——

I finally snarled loud enough to convince her; she rolled over on her back, and I had to pat her stomach to let her know we were still friends. With the canine equivalent of a shrug she started out.

She was gone for nearly ten hours.

"Dogs have no sense of time," I explained to Nina—possibly for the hundredth time.

She said reluctantly, "I know. I'm sorry if I'm pestering you. But I'm getting worried."

We had something to worry about, I agreed—but not out loud. I was the junior member of our expedition, and though we had never articulated a command relationship I was perfectly willing to treat Nina's "suggestions" as orders. Spying was her line of work, not mine. But it was dark. We were in enemy territory, and a good bet to be shot out of hand in case someone asked us questions. Our scout was overdue reporting back; and Nina was getting worried. And without any fuss, our relative positions changed; we were no longer commander and j.g., we were worried woman and—howsoever falsely—reassuring man. I liked it much better that way.

"Stay here. I'll take a look around," said the man to the woman.

"The devil you will," said the commander to the j.g. "Use your fat head for something, Logan. How do you expect to find the dog—whistle and clap your hands, all the way from here to the Caodai installation?"

I said reasonably: "Of course not. I just want to take a look around——"

"You said that. No."

So that was that—for the time being.

But time passed, and Josie stayed away; and what it came down to in the long run was the choice of which of us should go looking. And I won, if you can call it that.

Madagascar was an unfriendly place, after dark of a night; I could hear vehicles on the paved road—but I stayed off it; I could hear voices, now and again, around the houses that fronted on the river—but I gave them a wide berth. I felt something like a fawn somehow driven to slink through Central Park from end to end, avoiding the worrisome human smell from all about. Only I was more purposeful than a fawn, of course; closer perhaps to a beast of prey—say a fox, trying to raid a henhouse.

And unaware (or all too frighteningly aware) that the henhouse was guarded by mastiffs.

We had just about given up on Josie; I wasn't so much looking for the dog as trying to accomplish the dog's job. If Josie turned up where Nina waited in the clearing, good; Nina would hold her there until I returned. But if not, we could not stay there forever; it would then be my spied-out information we would go back to the whaleboat with, not Josie's. All I wanted was one clear look at the secret installation up ahead. Much more than that I couldn't hope for; but from whatever I could find out then, we could plan.

And I got my look at it.

There were lights ahead. I was on the brink of the woods, facing a plowed-up open strip that surrounded a lighted, barbed-wire-enclosed compound—the prison camps, I supposed. There were Caodai guards emplaced about the fence, but not so close to me that I had to worry about them; their attention would certainly all be in-ward, toward the prisoners. But beyond the barbed wire, perhaps a quarter of a mile, there were two brightly lit, yellow brick towers.

So far, so good. I skirted the edge of the plowed ground and headed for the lighted towers. I was pretty lucky. I must have got a hundred yards farther along before they caught me.

XV

"WESTERN SWINE!" hissed the Caodai. "Stay and brood on your crimes, Western swine!"

It didn't seem fair for him to call me that; he was as white as I. Fair-haired and chunky, he might have been of Dutch ancestry, but the Caodais didn't care about that.

He threw me into a cell and marched his detail away. I was in a yellow-walled room underneath the twin-towered building I had seen alight.

Logan, old boy, I told myself, you've had it. Consider the facts: I was out of uniform in Caodai territory—that made me a spy. It was well known what the Caodais did to spies; there had been grim stories.

There was only bright spot. Nina and Semyon were still free. They knew I had been captured, so they would be careful. Would being careful be enough? I didn't know, but, on thinking it over, I decided it wouldn't, because there simply was no precaution they could take that would counterbalance the fact that they *had* to penetrate the temple I was in.

I couldn't forget what the briefing officer had told us all, back on *Monmouth;* this expedition had to work, because the Caodais could not continue to be in possession of the secret of the Glotch.

"Western swine!"

My Dutch friend was at the door. He wasn't alone. A very dark Caodai, wearing a shoulder patch that looked like a rook in chess, brought in a case full of shiny things. Half a dozen other Caodais followed, and two of them grabbed me.

The dark one took a hypodermic needle out of the case.

"Wait a minute!" I said sharply. "You can't do this to me! I claim the protection of international law. You can execute me, but—ow!" He was mighty clumsy with that needle.

It tingled for a second, and then my whole upper arm

and shoulder began to feel cold. Well, I knew what was coming next. Subtle Oriental poisons, for a start. Then brainwashing. Torture.

I said to myself, Good-by, Elsie. I was beginning to feel cold all over; the fair-skinned Caodai was standing over me, but he seemed very far away.

He took out a pad of paper. "Your-name?" he demanded.

Name, rank and serial number. That was all, I reminded myself. I gave them to him as briskly and finally as I could: "Miller,,Logan, lieutenant junior grade, X-SaT-32880515."

"How did you get here?"

I stiffened; it was beginning. But he would never find out about *Monmouth* and the whaleboat from me. "I refuse to answer," I said distinctly.

It took an effort. The yellow walls were swirling around me now; I no longer felt cold, I hardly felt anything at all. I could barely hear the Dutch Caodai saying, "Where are your companions?"

Which one? Semyon was in the whaleboat, I supposed, but Nina— I got a grip on myself. "No answer," I said.

I stared at him blearily, wondering what made a man like him turn renegade. Of course, when the Caodais overran the former Dutch colonies in the Indies they had picked up everyone who would join them—in that respect the Caodais were a perfect democracy. But still and all, a white renegade in Caodai uniform was hard to take.

"Atheistic Western swine," hissed the Caodai, "don't dare call *me* a renegade!"

Fantastic, I thought to myself drowsily, it's almost as if I were speaking my thoughts aloud.

I woke up with a jump. I had a sour, tinny taste in my mouth, and an unbelievable headache.

Nina Willette was shaking me. "You cracked! Miller, listen to me."

I blinked blearily at her. She said, with pity and reproach: "They worked you over, didn't they, Logan? But you shouldn't have cracked."

119

"Hey," I said, "hold it!" I sat up and tried to set her straight. "I gave them my name and rank and serial number, right? That's all. I didn't crack!"

"No?" She looked at me, and the pity was subtracted from her gaze, leaving only the reproach. "Then how did they know where I was?"

I said, "Be reasonable, Nina, they must have——"

"How did they know *my name?*"

"My good God!" I whispered. "That needle. They must have shot me full of scopolamine . . ."

"Exactly, atheistic Western swine," said the blond Caodai, opening the door. "Exactly."

They were not gentle with us, but I hardly noticed. Truth serum! The psychic censors numbed, the questions answered—I must have spilled my guts for fair.

It was no comfort to reassure myself that it was not my fault. Because it was a lie. It *was* my fault; my fault for allowing myself to be captured, my fault for being there in the first place.

We were led out of the cell, Nina Willette and I, and up into the main workings of the twin-towered temple. Target Gamma! We were in the middle of it. If only we had some way of getting back to America with what we were seeing now!

And yet—and yet, coming blearily out of my fog of self-reproach, looking about me against the faint, almost vanished chance that I might some day be able to get back and report, what would I have said?

I could say: "We went through a long yellow corridor full of Caodais."

I could say: "They looked at us as though we were lepers."

But I couldn't say, for instance, that I had learned the secret of the weapon they called the Glotch, because there was no sign of anything like that anywhere around. An arsenal? I had thought we might be headed for something like that; but this didn't look like an arsenal. It looked more like a hospital, or perhaps a medical library, than anything else I had ever encountered, and that wasn't really a matter of looks but of smell, the faint underlayer of ether and iodoform you find in medical places. There were no whirring machines or hidden industrial plants, only the whispering air and medicinal odor and white-and-pastel look, in the little rooms we caught glimpses of.

And for this we had sacrificed *Monmouth.*

We reached a high-ceilinged room where an old Caodai in a scarlet cloak stood frozen beside a bright globe.

"Votre Sainteté," said the blond-haired Caodai, *"les américains."*

Nina stiffened beside me. "The pope," she whispered, unbelieving.

It took me a moment to understand what she meant. Not the pontiff of Rome, no, but the supreme chief of the Caodais, who wore the same title: The old Caodai by the globe of the world was Nguyen-Yat-Hugo himself!

Picture the Devil come to life.

Remember what I had seen of old Nguyen. Latrine posters, showing him luring helpless U.N. soldiery into haunts of bawdy vice, his yellow face wicked and fierce, his long fingers clawed like a killer cat's.

But he was only a man.

If he was evil, it did not show in his face. He stood gravely watching us as we approached. He was tall for an Indo-Chinese, old but not senile, his robes curious, but not ridiculous. I remembered the Caodais in their stockade north of Project Mako, and their fantastic paper figurines of this man. It was hard not to think of him as a figure of fun (Mardi gras masks and Jack-in-the-boxes), but in his presence it wasn't hard at all.

"You slime!"

Not evil but anger. He spoke to us, and he was raging. Nina, beside me, made a little choking sound. He lashed into us, cut us to ribbons. We were slime, wretches, unfit to live. We stood there and listened. What else could we do?

He finally rounded a period and stopped; and his face was as emotionless as before. He said something short and

121

foreign to one of the Caodai priests—a middle-aged woman who looked like my mother's laundress—and we all waited for a second while the priest left and returned.

When she returned she brought another woman with her, a slight brown-haired woman in faded khaki. I stared at her curiously as she blinked in the light. It crossed my mind that she was no Caodai. She had the look of an American, though her dress might have been Caodai as much as anything else. She looked out of place here. I watched her, waiting for something to happen that would explain why she was here.

By-and-by I noticed that the Caodais were watching me.

And then I realized who the girl was.

Strange? That I should see my long-lost wife and not at once recognize her?

I suppose so; but I wasn't the only one that had to do a double-take; Elsie didn't quiver a muscle until I yelled her name.

There was a dizzy, slippery, sliding moment when everything around me crashed into new arrangements and meanings and I stood still, like an idiot, bawling her name and staring. And then I was running toward her and she toward me, and——

We shook hands.

Call it that, anyway. At least it was more that than a lovers' hug. We stopped inches apart and I reached out my hands toward hers. It was a strained, formal moment. Perhaps the strain would have passed and we would have been in each other's arms, but the Caodai chief stopped us. "Your wife," he said in a clear, savage voice. "Enjoy her for this moment, my Lieutenant. She may not live to the next."

I had dropped Elsie's hands, spun around and was half-way to him, in a single reflex, before the Caodai officers brought me up. They were between me and Nguyen, and their weapons were in their hands. I stopped. I said, "What the devil are you up to?"

122

"Up to?" he repeated bitterly. "No, Lieutenant; I want to know what you are up to, not I. Perhaps we could have pieced out our information from your subconscious, where we found your wife's name and the story of your interesting voyage here. But it would have taken time, and I do not have time."

I took a deep breath, and the officers slowly holstered their guns. Nina was on one side of me and Elsie on the other. I said: "What do you want?"

"Information. Truthful answers, Lieutenant—for which I will pay, with your life and your wife's."

I glanced at Elsie and at Nina. Both of them were watching me, waiting for me to do something, waiting for my brilliant solution to an intolerable spot. But there wasn't any solution in me, search for it though I might. I looked around at the Caodai officers, at the implacable face of Nguyen-Yat-Hugo. The thing was bitterly ironic: the Caodai was demanding information from me, information that could hardly be of any real importance to the Caodai cause (for what did I have to say, past the minutiae of our voyage?), but which I knew I would die to keep from him. If our positions had changed their phase— if it were I who had the secret of what they called the Glotch, and he who had to learn it to live—then it might have made sense, both his insistence to learn, and my willingness to die, and have Nina and Elsie die, rather than tell. It didn't make sense; it was an outrageous perversion of human values for the three of us to suffer what was in prospect for the sake of concealing what little we had to conceal.

But that, as they say, was the way the little old ball bounced. I cleared my throat once and said to Nguyen-Yat-Hugo: "Go to hell!"

Well, the heavens didn't fall on us just then, though I had thought that they might. But I underestimated Nguyen.

All that happened was that he gave quick orders, and the three of us were marched out—separately. And there I was, in the yellow-walled room again. I knew what it

123

was, of course; the softening up that makes the ultimate tearing apart so much easier. Leave the Americans alone, Nguyen had said to his officers; put them away and let them worry for a while; let them scare themselves to death by brooding on what's going to happen to them.

But I didn't think it was going to work.

I sat there, staring at the yellow walls and wondering which of the footsteps in the corridor outside was going to be my torturer's, and I coded up all the factors and played them through the computer inside my skull. Too bad that I had spilled Elsie's name and location in my drugged state so that Nguyen could have her flown here to torture me with. Too bad that Nina had been caught the same way. Too bad that no one could get word of what had happened to us to Semyon, back in the whale-boat. Too bad, all of it too bad; but those losses were already raked in, and there was no point to wishing the little steel ball had dropped in a different slot.

It would have been better, I concluded, if I were in this all by myself, but since I wasn't I would have to do the best I could with the circumstances I had to work with. No matter what happened, Nguyen would roast in his Caodai hell before I would tell him a single syllable of what he wanted to know. Not because it mattered what I told him (for I knew nothing, of course), nor because I was a hero (for I knew from the shuddering of my arms and legs I was not); but because that was the way the game was played.

And I wasn't going to get out alive anyhow.

That was the important thing to remember: I was going to die. No matter what Nguyen said, I was a spy, trapped in a spy's role, and the best I could hope for was a quick firing squad.

Once I had thought out all of the possibilities the computer that was my brain quickly rapped out my solution; it wasn't hard to see. Back at M.I.T., when I had learned computer operation and the mathematics that went with it, we had had a course in what they call Theory of Games. It hadn't kept me from dropping all of my loose

124

change in each of the weekly poker nights; but it probably prolonged the process. Roughly it came to this: When things go well, play to win as much as you can; when things go poorly, play to lose as little. This was no spot for maximizing gains, there was no prospect of any gain worth having; it was a spot for minimizing losses. I couldn't hope to get us all freely and successfully away. But I could hope that, perhaps, I would be the only one to die. If I died, Nina would have to stand by herself— but was she any better off with me alive? And Elsie, on the other hand, was nothing to Nguyen. She had no information; she had not been trapped in espionage. Conceivably he might kill her out of pique—but not probably.

So the thing for me to do was to make the guards kill me right away.

On the principle of minimization of losses, I couldn't even try to grab a gun and shoot Nguyen; that was too risky—not to me, but to Elsie and Nina in case I was successful. What I had to have was a nice, quiet, futile attack on a humble, trigger-happy guard. End of Lieutenant Logan Miller. As minimal a loss as anyone could imagine.

I made my plans; and then I waited.

They came for me—I don't know after how long a time.

It was important that I do nothing premature. I didn't make the mistake of attacking them as soon as they poked their noses in the door—they might just have clobbered me with their fists, and tied me to make sure I didn't try it again. I went along with them. I hardly noticed them; I knew they were there, but I didn't understand a word they said, though I know the Dutch Caodai addressed me in English, I paid no attention to their actions or manner. Down the corridor, into the elevator, out into the great hall. At the entrance to the hall, I decided, I would grab for a gun, point it at the handiest figure in a yellow robe, and wait for the bullets.

It all went according to plan, or almost all. We got to the entrance, and the moment the door opened I made my move. I got the gun—surprisingly with no difficulty; I had thought that would be the hard part. But the guard's grip was incredibly lax. I had it and I leaped through the door and drew a bead on the female priest, the closest to me, standing morosely by the door. I could feel my shoulder blades drawing close to each other, waiting for the bullets to strike.

Only—no bullets.

Seconds passed. I gaped around. There were the Caodai officers, and there was Nguyen. And there, smoking a cigarette, swinging a gun in his free hand . . .

"Splendidly done, Logan!" applauded Semyon earnestly, throwing away the cigarette. "A brilliant maneuver; I should have known I would not be necessary. Is too bad you cannot capture these Orientals and deliver them to justice, is it not? But you see, I have done so already!"

XVI

IT TOOK a while for it to sink in.

Semyon shrugged modestly. "An heroic feat, you say?"

I hadn't said anything of the sort. "Oh, perhaps. But the credit should not merely be my own, Logan. Equally brave were the crew. We slipped up this filthy small river, every man at his post, searching out the Oriental target——"

I goggled. "What——"

"The *crew*," he said emphatically, "is brave also. Every *man* of them. No, no, Logan, I understand that you think of me as your rescuer, but without the six *men* in our crew out there in the river, *manning* the guns that will blow the roof off this very yellow brick building, what would my small gun accomplish?"

I caught on. He made it easy. I was surprised that Nguyen and his court didn't catch on, too; he made it so easy. But Semyon hurried on: "And we must not keep them waiting, Logan. If I do not appear outside within—" he consulted his watch "—eleven minutes, that is the end of all of us. Come, old man." He jerked his pistol at Nguyen. "Let us go to surrender."

Nguyen corrected coldly: "I agreed to talk. I do not surrender."

"Oh, let us have it as you wish, old man. But come outside now, if you please. Perhaps my crew's watches are not accurate."

Well, we all went—Semyon and the pope and Nina and Elsie, fresh from their own cells and as astonished as I. And then I was even more astonished; because just there, at the foot of the grass that went down to the little river, rocked the whaleboat, looking tiny and ridiculous in the African sun; and as we came out the muzzles of the deck guns, capable of launching high explosive shells that would blow us all to free ions in the air, swiveled to cover us.

127

I blinked at them incredulously; who were the gunners? And then I thought I understood. I whispered to Semyon: "Winnington?"

"Tied up," he whispered back. "Hush." Out loud he said: "What is it to be, old man? Do we all die here and now? Or do we discover a solution that permits us all to go on living?"

Nguyen, staring sourly at the little whaleboat, said: "There is none. You cannot go free. But it was clever of you, Lieutenant, to have lied under our drug."

I said helpfully, "Oh, I wasn't——"

"Enough!" cried Semyon. "One thing at a time, if you please." He glared at me. He said to the Caodai: "These are our terms. First, you give us safe conduct out of the belligerent zone. Second, you come with us as a hostage. Third, you attempt no reprisals. Fourth——"

"Three will do," said the Caodai. "No."

Semyon blinked at him. "No?"

"No." Nguyen was again the implacable, ageless figure I had first seen; he contemptuously ignored Semyon's gun, ignored the deck guns of the whaleboat, stepped close to Semyon and stared him in the eye. He said, "You shall not escape. You would not get so far as the mouth of the river."

Semyon said, "We'll blow you to bits."

"Do."

Impasse. Semyon looked at me. "Logan?" he inquired weakly.

I cleared my throat. "Will you give us a safe conduct, at least?"

"No."

"Will you——"

"No. Nothing, my Lieutenant. If the Great Palace wishes my death at this time, I shall die; that is as the Great Palace wishes it."

I stared at him thoughtfully. He stared right back, not giving an inch. It wasn't bluff. Here was the pope of all the Caodais, the supreme ruler of half the earth, the most deadly fighting man the world had ever made. And

128

here were we, a handful of unimportant humans and a couple of dogs and a seal, and he was willing to die rather than even to give us his promise—which he could have broken without a moment's pang—to let us go free. I shook my head silently. He never would have passed Game Theory at M.I.T., I thought sourly; everything was with him; this was a time for him to be maximizing his gains, stretching out to conquer the world, reeling under the Glotch. It was—it was——

I swallowed, and stared harder. Maybe, the thought came from nowhere, maybe he might have passed the course after all. Maybe it was not his technique that was wrong, but my estimate of the situation.

I contemplated the thought incredulously. Could it be, I asked myself, that things weren't going as well as they seemed for old Nguyen? It was ridiculous. And yet as he stood there he was no voracious conqueror; he was a sober, fierce old man, bedded to rock; hopeless of moving forward, but inflexibly unwilling to retreat.

It didn't make sense.

It was, as I say, an impasse, and we might have been there yet if Semyon had been brought up a Boy Scout. But he wasn't. And I don't know what they teach them at the Suvorov Academy, but I guarantee knot tying is not in the curriculum; because while we were staring at each other there was an interruption.

And the name of the interruption was Winnington.

It was Nina who saw him. "Logan!" she gasped. "We're in trouble!" And we were. The topside hatch of the whaleboat was open, and Winnington's surly face was staring out.

We were all armed, of couse, with guns we'd taken from the resentful Caodais, and perhaps if we'd been quicker we could get Winnington before he got out of the hatch. But he had the jump on us. He was out of the hatch and manning the deck guns from the breech position; and then it was too late. We couldn't shoot. If we had *looked* like we were going to shoot, it would have been the last look on the faces of any of us. He cut out

129

the switches to the remote fire control stations below and stared at us, collecting his thoughts.

A small brown pointed nose poked out of the hatch behind him. Josie. She looked worried, even at that distance; and I knew why. Semyon had left her to run the remotes on the deck guns, as she had so painstakingly learned back in the monitor at Project Mako; but his instructions had not included what to do in the event that the human captive got free. So Josie was perplexed.

But not so perplexed and worried as I, because I knew what Winnington was likely to do. Peace! He'd do whatever came to hand, for that unattainable ideal; he'd have peace if he had to blow up the world to get it.

He bent to the loud-hailer; his amplified bellow nearly bowled us over. "Get out of the way!" he roared.

Semyon shouted furiously: "Turn that thing off! Get away from those guns, Winnington, I command you!"

"Hah!" boomed Winnington; but he did, then, turn the loud-hailer off. "I said get out of the way!" he cried. "I see who you've got there. Either you move, or you go with him!"

And he put his thumbs on the trips.

Semyon choked: "Wait! Wait, Winnington! Let us not be hasty, there is much to lose." But he seemed to have panicked; he was snapping his fingers erratically, babbling words that made little sense. Winnington cried angrily: "No stalling, Timiyazev. I'll give you ten seconds to stand aside. Ten seconds, you hear me?"

"Please," begged Semyon, snapping his fingers frantically; I stared at him incredulously, wondering how far he had been pushed to dissolve so completely in panic. "Please, Winnington, I beg it of you, do not fire!"

And then I wasn't staring at Semyon at all, but at the deck of the whaleboat. Hesitantly, by fits and starts, looking bewilderedly at Semyon, Josie was moving up behind Winnington. It was absolutely impossible, I told myself, but she seemed to be following orders. But—what orders? I glanced at Semyon; he was scarcely looking at the dog, only pleading with the pacifist and snapping his——

130

Snapping his fingers.

I remembered the cricket, and the "leetle one-word language." And there, if you like, is a measure of comparative intelligence; for it was clear that Josie had remembered it before me. With the canine equivalent of a fatalistic shrug, she closed her eyes, leaned forward—and took a nip out of Winnington.

Reflexes are reflexes. Josie, yowling, was kicked yards away and into the water by Winnington's instinctive foot; but by the time Winnington got his eyes around front again it was a little too late. Semyon had been waiting; his gun was up; he fired; Winnington dropped.

"And now, old man," said Semyon, perfectly calm, "we resume our little talk—correct? I have saved your life. Be more reasonable now."

But Nguyen wasn't. He blazed: "Tricks, Russian! You have tricked me, I see, but it is not important. If I must die, I die gladly, for I have no wish to outlive the Great Palace. If the world cannot be Caodai, let me perish!"

There it was again! Even Semyon blinked.

Nguyen was roaring on: "Name your conditions, I refuse them all. Filth and slime, killers, vermin! You have us, but I spit on you!"

Semyon glanced at me.

It was my turn to argue with Nguyen. But I didn't do it. There was a sudden queer flash, quick and gone.

Elsie put her hand on my arm. "What—what—" It had been like lightning, but there were no clouds; I couldn't understand it.

But Semyon understood it; Semyon understood it very well. He moaned something in Russian, his face gone suddenly sick. He nodded to me and said, conversationally, "The clouds again, you see, Logan. Climbing like trees on the horizon." That was silly, because I had just looked and there weren't any clouds, not one.

No.

There hadn't been any clouds. But now there was one.

"Like Irkutsk once more," said Semyon, and gestured with his gun to the horizon. I looked, incredulous, as the mounting cloud leaped and spread; and then the concussion hit us from the distant nuclear blast.

XVII

WE NESTLED on the bottom, a mile off shore, and waited. Waited for what? Not for some miracle to put fuel in our tanks, for there was no hope of that; not for someone to rescue us, for the U.N. would never come near Madagascar and the Caodais would not rescue but kill. Not even for the world to come to an end. For that had already begun. We just waited.

. Semyon was comforting the animals; Elsie and Nina were sitting inspecting each other in silence. We had taken a prisoner, old Nguyen himself, and he was bound where once we had bound the late pacifist, Winnington. Too bad he was dead, I told myself, he would have been delighted with the way things were working out. Because the pacifist dream, the war to bring peace by destroying all warriors, was already well begun.

Nguyen said heavily from his corner, "Incredible." He was staring reflectively at Semyon and the dogs. "They are your animals; you use them as slaves. Some you kill and eat, do you not? The Caodai does not eat flesh, that seems horrible to us. And yet—they love you."

Semyon patted Josie. "We love them!" he said defiantly. Nguyen shrugged.

"It is well known," he said, "that you love everyone and everything. It accounts for the satellite bombings as easily as for your slaughterhouses."

"Shut up, old man!" said Semyon. He crooned to the dogs, while Elsie flared up:

"Put a gag in his mouth. I'm sick of Caodai hypocrisy. The Western atheists do this and the Western atheists do that, and there we are moldering away in their prison camps, while they pretend that the fault's all ours. Gag him! Or I'll shut him up myself."

I looked in some amazement at my warrior bride.

For I remembered Elsie. She was a quiet and biddable girl when we married—not counting her habit of volun-

133

teering, of course. I'd never heard her shout at anyone—not at anyone at all, not even me. True, Nguyen was the arch-enemy, and she must have had pitiful fantasies of a chance like this while she was in the concentration camp. But—even so.

Not the least of the problems of the big cold war, I thought, would come when the Elsies and the Mes tried to get back to where we could recognize each other again.

Nina Willette was collecting herself again. She was an intelligence officer, and she too had no doubt had ridiculous dreams of a chance like this. "Now then!" she said briskly to the pope of the Caodai. "Tell me what you were doing here."

He looked at her calmly. "I ask you to tell me," she wheedled. "Please. There is no use to keep a secret, is there?" She offered him a cigarette and smiled, woman-to-man.

"An admirable performance," commented Nguyen. "I do not smoke, but your interrogation is splendid."

"Thank you. Why did you leave Cambodia for this lousy little island?" He shrugged. Nina smiled again. "Good," she said. "You stick to your principles. I don't suppose any of us will last twenty-four more hours, but we might as well go on with it, just as if it mattered whether you gave up information, or I obtained it. So I shall continue to ask questions, and you will answer only where it doesn't matter. Correct?"

Nguyen said heavily, "Correct."

Semyon cut in, "You could at least tell us what is happening, old man. There is no secret about that."

Nguyen closed his eyes. "The end of the world is happening. Your ship attacked us in our own waters. We retaliated. Your people retaliated against our retaliation——"

"The satellite bombs?"

"You have seen one of them," said Nguyen-Yat-Hugo. "You must realize that our bombs are falling too."

Nina whimpered, "But why? You must have known it was the end for all of us!"

134

Semyon raged: "Couldn't you wait, old man? Your weapon was too slow, was it? The burning and killing did not satisfy you, you must unleash the satellite bombs——"

Nguyen said hoarsely, "A moment. Our weapon? What weapon is that?"

"I do not know your name for it," Semyon said in contemptuous tones. "We call it the Glotch; it is a burning fire that strikes the head and neck and——"

He trailed off. The stern, stiff old face of Nguyen was cracking. "No," said Nguyen, shaking his head.

It was incredible, but you couldn't doubt the expression on his face. I stammered, "It—it isn't your weapon?"

"It is *not*," said Nguyen with passion. "The Caodai is on its knees beneath it!"

We stared at each other. If it wasn't a Caodai weapon and Elsie confirmed that it had struck the Caodais as hard as us—and if it wasn't our own weapon, which it was not——

Whose weapon was it?

"Too late, too late!" whispered Nguyen, looking through our periscopic sights. We had surfaced, and the smoking coast of Madagascar was a mile or less away.

"Maybe the damage is only local," I said. "Can you raise anyone on the radio, Nina?"

She shook her head. "Everybody's jamming," she said briefly.

"Fall-out negligible," Semyon reported from the aft lookout ports. "There must have been an offshore wind. One should not swim too long in these waters, though."

I said to the pope of the Caodai: "If we find a spot on the coast where we can safely land, can you conduct us to a place where we can radio the U.N. forces?"

He spread his hands, his face a mask. "I can try."

"We haven't any other choice, Logan," Elsie reminded me. I noticed that her hand was in mine. Even if we could refuel this boat, we could scarcely navigate it back across the Atlantic."

"Man your stations," I ordered. "Nguyen, I assume you

135

haven't any hailing signal we could use for a safe-conduct? It would be a help, if a Caodai ship should spot us——" He shook his head.

"Full speed south then," I said. "As long as the fuel holds out."

It held out better than I had expected; we made nearly ten miles before the engines began to splutter. While we still had steerage way I spun the rudder wheel, and we slanted in on a sandy beach. There were concrete pill-boxes and *chevaux-de-frise*, and God knows how many electronic and sonar alarms we triggered as we beached. But there apparently were very few Caodais at the filter centers that day, after the bombs had fallen. Our only real danger—from that particular source, at least—was that someone would notice we had landed on a radar remote, and send over a nike to home in on us to save the trouble of investigating.

We ran away from the beach, as far as we could get before our breath ran out, in case a wandering patrol should happen by.

"There is," said the pope, "a command post somewhere about. I consecrated it myself, two days ago."

We sent one of the monkeys up a tree, but she either couldn't understand what we wanted, or her short simian vision didn't let her detect the building we had described. Semyon, cursing in Russian, tried climbing it himself. But we couldn't get high enough to see, any of us.

"It is this way," said Nguyen strongly, and what could we do but follow his lead?

And he led us right into a trap.

There were Caodais all over the place. They swarmed from the command post like termites from a hill; there was a rattle of small arms fire, and rushing brown-skinned men in uniforms, and it was all over before we could move. For a moment when they jumped us I had old Nguyen in front of my gun, and I don't know why I didn't pull the trigger. "Treacherous beast," sobbed Semyon, "we trusted you and you betrayed us!" And I felt much the same.

136

"No!" cried Nguyen, and he bellowed something at the Caodai soldiers. They gave him an argument. Apparently he wasn't recognized; but they took us all to the command post, and there was a long, complicated discussion in French too fast for my ears. Nina, following it as closely as she could, explained:

"They don't know him. They think he's an impostor, and the fat one is all for shooting the lot of us. Now somebody's going to get a picture, and then——"

They brought the picture—a ceremonial portrait draped in yellow bunting, as remote a likeness to the real man in its own prettifying way as the caricatures in our latrines had been in theirs.

But it convinced them; and that was that. So all we had to do was arrange to use their radio, get in touch with the U.N. command in Washington, stop the war and clear up the mess.

It was a tough assignment. All the more because we never got past Step One. Jamming loud and furious—jamming by the Caodais and jamming by us. There were no radio communications anywhere, period.

XVIII

Not only were we the ones who were trying to stop the war, it looked as though we had started it. For the naval action that *Monmouth* precipitated had spread. The Caodais had sunk her. A U.N. fleet had made a daring raid into interdicted waters to try to rescue her. In retaliation, the Caodais had raided the Caribbean again. In retaliation for that, a strike against Cebu. In retaliation for that—it had wound up with the satellite bombs.

We looked at the situation map in the radio room, and it was like the end of the world. There had been at least eighty fusion bombs dropped.

And a weary, jittery black radioman in a Caodai uniform was trying to get through with the message that might stop it all; but it was hopeless. He glanced at us and shrugged. "*Je m'y perds, votre Sainteté,*" he said. "*Je ne puis pas.*"

Nguyen said heavily: "He cannot get through."

A *sous-tenente* who spoke fair English cleared his throat and said: "Sir, perhaps if we have patience a time will come when we can get through. There have been breaks in the jamming; we received messages for nearly half an hour this morning."

"No. There will be no more breaks—except as the stations are bombed off the air." He smiled wryly. "It is that which we wish to prevent."

Semyon looked up from the animals. "Fantastic," he said, his eyes round. "It is not your weapon. It is not our weapon. But we bomb each other."

Nina Willette was still an intelligence officer. She asked: "Have you really lost many to this burning thing? I suppose I can't call it the 'Caodai Horrors' any more."

Nguyen hesitated only a moment. Then he rapped out: "More than seven hundred thousand. Nearly every one of our—what is your word—our telepathists; and a few others. And you?"

It was Nina's turn to hesitate. Still, he had been frank with her, or had seemed to. "I'm not sure. But perhaps half a million."

Half a million! Semyon and Elsie and I stared back and forth among ourselves. So many, I thought; how can there have been so many? But the more I thought, the more plausible it got. For even in my own small experience there had been half a dozen or more. Half a million; one out of every five hundred or so on the North American continent.

Elsie, surprisingly, grinned; and in that moment she was my Elsie again. She took my hand. "No more calling up your wife just to see how she is, Logan. It's too expensive now—if this thing knocks off the espers, they'll raise their rates. Is it always espers?"

"All," said Nguyen. "Nearly all professionals, and a few others who had recently been sensitized. And with you?"

"I think so," said Nina. "You understand that it was a highly classified matter with us—but I think so."

"So you see?" Elsie clutched my hand. "From now on, esping will be purely on matters of the gravest importance—on matters—on——"

She stared at me, then wordlessly at the useless radio.

"On matters, she proclaims, of the gravest importance!" howled Semyon. "But surely! They cannot jam the telepathic waves, however hard they try. It is our way to reach America!"

Our way to reach America.

But we didn't have an esper at hand to do it.

Nguyen sent scouts racing across the Madagascan littoral in all directions; and they came back with psychologists, with Caodai military communications men, with a mixed bag of assorted protesting black, brown and yellow men and women. But not an esper in the lot.

Nguyen snapped: "If you had not killed them off——" He flushed. "My apology. If they had not *died* through this thing we both wish to combat, it would be easy. But

139

there is scarcely a telepathist in all the lands of the Great Palace. Hardly even a man who was sensitized, much less an expert."

Elsie looked at me and shook her head sharply. But all the same I cleared my throat and said:

"I was sensitized only a few weeks ago."

"I was sensitized last year," Nina Willette said suddenly. No one else said anything at all.

Then Elsie burst out: "That's ridiculous, Logan! You're no esper, you only paid your money to *use* one. Good heavens, I was part of the same hookup, so if you——"

"I was sending," I told her. "You were only receiving."

She said desperately, "But Logan! It's dangerous; you heard what this man said; it's bad enough in America, but in Caodai territory esping is a quick way to die. Don't do it! Let that girl try——"

Then she looked me in the eye and stopped. "I'm sorry, darling," she said after a moment.

"I was sensitized more recently, dear," I mentioned to her.

Wearily: "I know."

"It, uh, it probably isn't really dangerous. I still have my helmet. I'll just take it off to see if I can reach some American esper. Then as soon as I've got through——"

"I know." She reached up and kissed me, hard. Then she turned away. "Get on with it," she said over her shoulder . . .

We talked to one of the psychologists Nguyen's patrols had rounded up, a faded tan-skinned man with a bulbous face and a thin black mustache, who claimed to know a little about the theory of ESP. The *sous-tenente* translated· "You cannot reach anyone except a trained esper or one with whom you have a had a—a—excuse, but what is the English word for *rapport*."

" 'Rapport.' Get on with it," said Nina impatiently.

The *sous-tenente* pursed his lips. "Curious. Well then, you must try to reach someone with whom you have formerly been in contact. Preferably an esper, if there is one. Think of him, and of the place where you saw him last, and of the sounds and smell of the room; recreate it all in your mind. But do not linger on a single person, for perhaps he is dead. Try one as best you can; if no answer, try another. You comprehend?"

"I comprehend," I said. "Let's go."

We went to work.

We took off our aluminum helmets—that I for one had lived in, slept in, even bathed in for weeks. We lay down on hard cots in a room of the command post, and they closed the door.

And then we tried to telepath.

It was a funny sensation—something like trying to flex the fingers on a third hand. I was straining muscles that didn't exist, reaching through the void with members I did not own, shouting with vocal chords that should have been in the base of my skull, and were not. In the hands of the esper it had been quick and easy. There was the gray wandering and the sense of touching, and there was a contact.

Now—nothing. We lay there like a pair of idiots. Could we ever reach anyone? Ridiculous, I thought. Could a jellyfish solve quadratic equations? The brain tissue, whatever it was that held the ESP-power, simply did not exist in us; we were not espers.

I belligerently followed directions, daring something to happen. I thought of Giordano and his office on the Venetian Causeway. Nothing.

I thought of the smell of rotting palm trees and hibiscus, the warmth of the early summer Miami air, the way his breath had rasped as he was helping me reach Elsie . . .

Nothing.

All right, I said, I give up; I thought of another esper, the one in Providence . . .

And I got Giordano.

Peevishly: *Who the hell are you? Don't you know this is dangerous?*

Not words, of course. I've explained that esping is not

a matter of words. But an irritation, and a question, and a warning.

I tried—as a blind castaway might try to spot a sail on the horizon—I tried, ineptly and without knowing whether I was succeeding, to convey what I had to say. The Glotch is not a Caodai weapon. It kills them as well as us. Tell the high command. Tell them to stop the bombs. The Caodai didn't start the war. They are dying as rapidly as we. Stop it, stop it, until we find out . . .

Until, finally, an incredulousness from Giordano, an understanding, at last a belief, and a promise. I could almost see him, seated at his desk, not in Miami now but in some colder, drier place, staring at emptiness, conversing with me. He was nodding, promising . . .

Bright yellow fireflies came between us.

I shook my head, and the rapport was gone. No more Giordano; no more sense of touch.

But the fireflies were still there. Fire lanced through the base of my neck. I yelled out loud, and clawed for the helmet I had dropped beside my cot. The pain was terrible, worse than that night along the drive at Miami Beach, worse than anything I had ever felt. I got the helmet and jammed it onto a head filled with hurting and flame. "Help!" I bawled; and I wondered if the door was really opening, if people were really bursting in, if that was really Elsie clutching me in her arms. My head rolled to one side, and I caught a glimpse of the cot next to mine. There was something there, something that had been a person; but it wasn't Nina Willette; not with blackness and horror where the pretty young face had been, not with the charred agony that was crisped into the expression. Nina Willette? Preposterous! It was a seared corpse, it couldn't be she!

But it was, all the same. So I found out—more than a week later, when they dared take the needles out; when they had stopped enough of the pain and patched enough of the ruin around my head and neck, and began to think I might yet live—the only man in all the world who had

142

survived not a single attack of whatever-it-was, but two.

And Elsie was there.

We didn't talk for a while; and then we talked. The war was over; I had after all got through, and so had Nina—before she died. It was good that we both made it, for they would scarcely have believed one. But you do not lie through ESP, and two of us could hardly be mistaken.

So they had stopped the bombs, and the satellites hung silent in the sky. And the Caodais and we had begun to compare notes and to look for answers. Volunteers had offered themselves as sacrifice—some had died, sitting in darkened rooms with opened photographic shutters waiting to catch the track of whatever came flashing in as they esped; a few coughing their lungs out in improvised cloud chambers; a great many were surrounded by infinite varieties of scientific equipment that tasted and measured and felt.

After a day I was well enough to walk about. The grafts from the skin bank were healing, and the damage to the nervous system was slight. And I had a visitor. I was in a naval hospital outside of what had been New Washington, and there Nguyen had flown to sign the Bethesda Compact. And he came to see me and to say, "Thank you."

That was the greatest shock of all. "For what?" I demanded.

Nguyen laughed silently. "We are in your debt, my Lieutenant," he said. "We have learned to get along together, the Caodai and the West, and that is good. And even more, through your work with the dogs and monkeys and seals, we have learned to get along with our animals. And only just in time, my Lieutenant. Only just in time."

He was in earnest. "In time for what?" I asked.

He said: "What you call the Glotch. It wasn't our weapon or yours. In fact, you see, it was not a weapon at all. Today the news is made: It is life."

143

I stared. *"Life?"*

He nodded heavily. "Living things. Telepathic. Tiny. Below the threshold of visibility. They seek to communicate when they sense the subtle esper flow; and because their structure and ours cannot exist together—they die. And perhaps that could be borne, but we die too. As you know."

"Life!" I breathed. "How on earth——"

"Ah, no!" he cried. "Not on earth at all. Mars? I don't know—but not on earth, that is sure. And that is why we were only just in time. For now that we have learned to get along with each other—we start, this second, to learn to get along with Them. They have been attracted from outside, the scientists think, by our esping and our bombs. I doubt they will ever leave us alone again."

"Mars!" I breathed. It was fantastic.

And also, of course, wrong—but how thoroughly wrong we did not discover for some months after, until Venus once more swam into close approach to the earth.

But that's another story.

A NOTE ABOUT THIS BOOK

IT IS NOT the business of a science-fiction writer to record matters of contemporary fact or scientific truths which have already been discovered. It is his business to take what is already known and, by extrapolating from it, draw as plausibly detailed a portrait as he can manage of what tomorrow's scientists may learn . . . and of what the human race in its day-to-day life may make of it all.

Since not all of *Slave Ship*'s scientific elements are "extrapolations," it seems worthwhile to set down a rough guide to which is which. To the best of the author's knowledge, no human being since Dr. Doolittle has been able to conduct a conversation on any abstract subject with any creature or thing other than another human being. However, animal languages do exist—not merely among the geniuses of the animal kingdom such as primates and dogs, but as far down among the phyla as one cares to go. The question, of course, turns upon the definition of the term "language." Bees have been clearly demonstrated to communicate with sets of signals, for example. If one allows only a "spoken" language, we turn to the frog, perhaps the lowest animal to have a voice at all: A species of frog from Santo Domingo owns at least one "word," a sort of pig-squeal alarm cry utterly different from its normal barking sound.

Progressing to higher orders, Dr. Konrad V. Lorenz is perfectly able to communicate, on such matters as would interest them, with jackdaws, with mallards and with greylag geese, among others. His command of the Jackdaw language, for example, includes such subtleties as the two forms of the verb "to fly"—*Kia*, to fly away; *Kiaw*, to fly back home. Other persons, working with other birds, have achieved successes of their own. Ernest Thompson Seton recorded a long list of "words" in

145

Crow; a scientist prepared a seven word "dictionary" of Rooster; etc.

When we come to the mammals, we might expect to find considerable increases both in the number of "words" and in the sophistication with which they are used. We will not be disappointed. It is hard to imagine a man who has lived for any length of time in intimate contact with a dog, for instance, who will deny that his dog has sought communication with him and sometimes attained it. It is true that domesticated animals (particularly when they are so thoroughly domesticated as the dog) are a special case—it is as though an American child were brought up in Babylon; he would undoubtedly learn to communicate, but it would be in Babylonian terms and not in the language he had been born to. It is worth observing that at least one dog—his name was Fellow, and he was an honored guest at Columbia University in New York—had a vocabulary in English of *four hundred* words, which he recognized regardless of who spoke them. But we must strike Dog from our list as, at best, a sort of *beche-la-mer* or pidgin, thoroughly contaminated with Human.

Cat might be purer—and some fifteen words of Cat have been identified, along with some six words of Horse and a few each of Elephant and Pig. But the linguists of the animal kingdom, at least in their own and native tongues, are the primates. The gibbon, the gorilla and the orangutan have notable vocabularies; and the chimpanzee, best studied of primates short of man, not only has a vocabulary of some thirty-two distinct words, according to Blanche.Learned, but may have a unique claim to linguistic fame. A philologist named George Schwidetzky believes he has found traces of Chimpanzee loan-words in ancient Chinese ("ngak"), in a South African Bushman dialect (a tongue click), and even in modern German! (The German word, "geck," derived from Chimpanzee "gack.")

One definition of Man calls him "the tool-using animal" —yet elephants crop tree branches to swat flies, spider monkeys construct vine ladders for their young, and there is some plausible evidence that the polar bear hunts sleeping walruses with the aid of that primitive tool, the missile, in the form of a hurled chunk of ice. Another definition identifies Man as "the linguistic animal"—but even the few remarks above will indicate that that claim is far less than unique.

Perhaps there is room for a third definition of Man, not much better than the other two, but very likely not much worse: Man, the snobbish animal . . . who clings to evolution's ladder one rung higher than the brutes beneath and saws away, saws away at the ladder beneath in an attempt to sever the connection between himself and the soulless, speechless, brainless Beast . . . that does not, in fact, exist.

ABOUT THE AUTHOR

Frederik Pohl, at thirty-seven, has published twenty-two books, but *Slave Ship* is his first full-length science-fiction novel which was not written in collaboration—usually with C. M. Kornbluth. Apart from the Pohl-Kornbluth stories (*The Space Merchants, Search the Sky, Gladiator-at-Law*), Mr. Pohl is best known in the science-fiction field for the seven highly praised anthologies he has edited (including the *Star Science Fiction Stories* series of collections of originals) and for his own short stories, the first collection of which in book form was *Alternating Currents*. A former editor, literary agent and advertising executive, Mr. Pohl has now settled down to a career of full-time writing in his home on the New Jersey shore where he lives with his wife and three children.

Date Due

CPSIA information can be obtained
at www.ICGtesting.com
Printed in the USA
BVHW050804140223
658473BV00005B/144

9 781013 875830